PRAISE FOR B.M. ALLSOPP'S SERIES

FIJI ISLANDS MYSTERIES

Death of a Hero: How it all began *(Prequel novella)*
Readers' reactions in Amazon customer reviews

'I can honestly say that I was hooked from the first page!'

'I love Allsopp's writing: plot-line, characterization, well-researched details, settings - all are excellent. And the characters are not just believable, they are so well written you feel like you know them personally.'

'All fans of Horseman have to enjoy this deeper look into Joe's reasons for joining the police force. And as always, a close and gentle look into Fijian culture. Well done!'

'This is a fast-paced mystery that will keep readers guessing. If you've never read any books in this series, this is a great place to start. If you are already a fan, here's a look back at a young Horseman. Enjoy!'

'I enjoyed learning the back-story on Joe Horseman. A great addition to the series. 5 Stars!'

Death on Paradise Island
'A refreshing take on the crime novel' - lrina Dunn, Director, *Australian Writers Network*

'This is a superb debut novel, which I enjoyed hugely. I look forward very much to seeing more in the *Fiji Islands Mysteries* Series." - *Sisters in Crime Australia*

This debut novel, has excellent balance between plot, character and setting. The plot is nicely twisty. The main characters are strongly executed… There's a tremendous sense of place and culture…It's cleverly done, most observation is through the eyes of the local hero, recently returned, with no rose-coloured glasses in sight. Definitely a series to keep an eye on. ' - Karen Chisholm, *AustCrimeFiction.org*

'The author evidently knows Fiji and its people intimately. But instead of being just a palm-trees and coral sands backdrop, the Fijian natural and human environment is an integral part of the story. All these facets are so well integrated that I felt the plot really belonged with the setting, as did the characters.' - Prof. Ian Campbell, author of *Worlds Apart: A History of the Pacific Islands*

Death by Tradition

'What really hooked me was the setting. The heat and humidity steam off the page… *Death by Tradition* is a damn good read and will appeal to readers who enjoy a story rich in setting and who also delight in those little

'Wow, I didn't know that!' moments.' - *Sisters in Crime Australia*

'As with the first novel in this series, the sense of culture and place is incredibly strong. The deeply traditional beliefs and lifestyle of this village contrast interestingly with the holiday resort setting from the first novel as well... I particularly like the way that there are such views of a very different way of life...' - Karen Chisholm, *AustCrimeFiction.org*

Death beyond the Limit
Advance Readers' reactions

'The book got off to a really fast start – it just jumped out and grabbed my attention – it's really hard to top finding a human head in a shark's belly! I had a hard time putting this book down, and ended up reading until all hours of the night to finish it. enjoyed the very clever solution to the story. Bravo!!! I think it's going to be hard to top this book!'

'The latest book (in the series) was superb. I couldn't put it down.'

'The relentless pursuit to solve the mystery of the severed head...kept me captivated the entire two days it took me to finish it.'

(The author) 'has done a huge amount of research for this, and it pays off.'

EXCLUSIVE TO MY READERS

It's wonderful getting to know my readers. One of the best things I've learned is that you are just as fascinated by the lovely islands of Fiji as I am. If you enjoy this book, I invite you to join B.M. Allsopp's Readers.

As a welcome gift, I'll present you with something new (and free) to read that you won't find in any book store. I'll tell you more after you've finished ***Death of a Hero***.

ALSO BY B.M. ALLSOPP

Death on Paradise Island
Death by Tradition
Death Beyond the Limit

B.M. ALLSOPP

DEATH
OF A HERO

Fiji Islands Mysteries: How it all began
A prequel novella

Coconut Press

Paperback edition first published in Australia in 2020
by *Coconut Press*
Copyright © B.M. Allsopp 2019
ISBN 978-0-6488911-2-3

E-book first published in Australia in 2019
by *Coconut Press*
Copyright © B.M. Allsopp 2019
www.bmallsopp.com
Contact the author by email at
bernadette@bmallsopp.com
Kindle ISBN 978-0-9945719-6-0
Epub ISBN 978-0-9945719-7-7

A catalogue record for this
work is available from the
National Library of Australia

To all my former students at the
University of the South Pacific.

THE PRINCIPAL ISLANDS OF FIJI

AUTHOR'S NOTE: The village of Tanoa is fictitious, as are Paradise and Delanarua islands. Other places on this map are real, but nearly 300 exquisite small islands are omitted.

GLOSSARY AND GUIDE TO
FIJIAN PRONUNCIATION

I use a few basic Fijian greetings and polite
expressions in my books to give readers a
taste of an intrinsic part of Fijian culture.
You may also be interested to know how to
pronounce the names of people and places
in the stories.

bula — hello
moce — goodbye or goodnight
io — yes
vakalevu — very much
vinaka — thank you
yaqona — kava (the plant *piper methysticum*:
its roots, ground powder and drink)

Spelling

The Fijian alphabet is based on English but it is phonetic, so each sound is always represented by only one letter, unlike English.

Vowels

a as in *father*
e as in *met*
i as in *Fiji*
o as in *or*
u as in *flu*

Consonants

Most consonants are pronounced roughly as in English, with the following important exceptions.

b = *mb* as in me*mb*er eg. **b**ula = **mb**u-la
d = *nd* as in te*nd*er eg. **d**ina = **nd**i-na
g = *ng* as in si*ng*er eg. li**g**a = li-**ng**a
q = *ngg* as in stro*ng*er eg. ya**q**ona = ya-**nggo**-na
c = *th* as in mo*th*er eg. ya**c**o = ya-**th**o

MONDAY

1

Josefa Horseman ripped the team's training singlets from the washing line, gave the orange tree a good shake, tossed the fallen fruit into the kit bag with the other gear and took off. He dashed down the steep shortcut from the student dormitories to the rugby field. Seru would not be happy if he was late with the gear. Neither would Horseman himself. He was honoured Seru had entrusted him with this job for the team.

Relieved to be the first to arrive for training, he went to the water tap stand first and filled the containers, leaving two beside the tap. He took the other two over to the changing shed, which for some reason was positioned on the opposite side of the field from the tap. You'd think the administrators of the University of the South Pacific, all rugby devotees, would provide more taps for their own teams, wouldn't you?

Horseman dumped the kit bag and water containers beside the door, went back to the tap and returned with the remaining two. He opened the door, pushed back an ill-fitting wooden shutter and looked for the coconut broom which he'd left leaning in a corner. Instead of a broom, a tall man was sitting there, his face slumped to his chest. Seru had got here first after all. This was either a trick or he'd gone to sleep.

'*Bula*, hello Seru.' Horseman wanted to save his captain embarrassment. He repeated his greeting more loudly. He went up to Seru, touched his arm, shook his shoulder gently, then more firmly, calling his captain's name again and again. But Seru's big, handsome head rolled further forward. Alarm seized Horseman but he remembered his first aid training. He raised Seru's legs, propped them up against the wall, and lowered his body to the cement floor, willing him to come out of his faint. Seru was still, too still. When Horseman realised Seru wasn't breathing, he checked his wrist, then his neck, for a pulse. Was he imagining the faintest, uneven beat? The pounding of his own heart against his rib cage distracted him.

He had to get help. No one else had arrived yet. He'd better run up to the dormitory to call an ambulance on the public phone. He was nearly there when he realised USP's own medical clinic was only fifty metres further. He must calm down and think coolly.

He barged into the clinic, yelling 'Emergency!' to the receptionist, who froze. He banged on the doctor's door, then flung it wide. Dr Koroi leapt to her feet.

'You can't just…'

'Just come! The captain's collapsed at

the rugby field. No breathing, no pulse. Please!'

Dr Koroi took one sharp look at him and grabbed a bag. She turned to her patient, 'Sorry, it's an emergency. I must go'.

As they hurried out, she shouted to the receptionist, 'Call an ambulance to the rugby field, please. Reschedule my appointments.' Hope surged through Horseman as he led her down the slope.

By the time Dr Koroi shook her head regretfully at Horseman, half the players had turned up for training. Dr Koroi forbade anyone but Horseman to enter the shed so they milled about outside, anxious and baffled.

'We must wait for the ambulance,' she said to Horseman.

Thank God, those faint, spasmodic pulses hadn't been imagination. His own heart raced again. 'Seru's unconscious then, Doctor? He'll recover in hospital?'

Her wide brown eyes looked directly into his, sympathetic. 'Unless I'm very much mistaken, Seru has already died.'

'How? Why? What happened?' Horseman clutched his head to stop it spinning.

'I'm afraid I don't know yet, but we'll find the answer, I assure you.'

Horseman staggered out the door, away from her words. 'Seru's dead,' he blurted.

The players moved in, linking arms, forming a circle. Some rubbed tears away, others let them run freely, yet others, dry-eyed, looked blank. A baritone started singing softly, then other voices joined in four-part natural harmonies. They all knew the 23rd Psalm. When they reached "*I will fear no evil*", their young voices strengthened in a crescendo of confidence.

2

The ambulance team had called the police and now stood back while the blue uniforms shooed the rugby players away, staked out an area around the shed, and wound blue and white tape around it. Their coach, Professor Lakepi Hau'ofa of the Fiji School of Medicine, had already joined Dr Koroi and been permitted to remain in the shed with her. The officers now raised the tape for a lanky sandy-haired European man carrying a toolbox. Three more Fijian men with an air of authority about them unhooked the tape and joined the others in the shed.

Horseman was dizzy. Who were all

these people? Of course, he recognised the police and ambulance uniforms, but the others? Now four more, all in sky blue overalls, were admitted to the enclosure but waited outside the shed, talking among themselves. Horseman turned to the team-mate next to him.

Before he could ask, his friend explained. 'They're SOCOs, scene-of-crime officers.'

'Crime? What crime?'

'None, I hope! When there's a sudden unexplained death, the police call the SOCOs in to collect any clues, like fingerprints, if they're suspicious.'

'Suspicious of what?'

'Well, that the death is not natural. Haven't you seen any cop shows on TV? Wait, here's Coach now. And Dr Koroi.'

Their coach walked into the circle. Professor Hau'ofa had played for Tonga in more than a hundred rugby internationals over 15 years. All the USP team were proud he was their coach.

'Boys, boys, what can I say? However

much we wish it were not so, our much-esteemed first grade captain, Seru Namata, has passed away quite unexpectedly. I thank our youngest and newest team member, Joe Horseman, who found Seru and quite correctly fetched Dr Koroi. Tragically, Joe was too late.'

Half the team turned to stare at Horseman. Did he imagine some suspicious faces? Surely Coach had not implied Horseman was to blame for Seru's death. If he'd arrived ten minutes earlier, would Seru have lived?

'Yes, I know all of us are experiencing shock, so I'll cancel training this afternoon. However, our Seru would want us to win Saturday's game against Police. So we'll meet tomorrow at the same time for an extra session and Thursday training as normal, no matter how sad we're feeling.'

Horseman nodded, others muttered their agreement. Two of the men came out of the shed and approached them. Coach turned as he noticed the team's attention was distracted.

'Ah, Detective Sergeant, have you something to say to the boys?'

The shorter of the two men nodded and stepped forward. His round face made him look younger than he probably was, an impression reinforced by his camouflage cargo pants and baseball cap.

'I am Detective Sergeant Ratini. This is my colleague Detective Constable Taleca.' He indicated his tall, skinny companion, who nodded to them in a friendly way. 'He'll speak to all of you students, then you should leave and let us get on with our job. Except for the boy who discovered the body.' Horseman winced at the officer's casual use of the word *body*. He raised his hand.

Coach intervened, beckoning Horseman forward with his chin. 'Detective Sergeant, this is Josefa Horseman, my youngest player. You will understand he's somewhat shocked.'

DS Ratini's smile was a grim stretch of his mouth. 'Aha, your latest prodigy, Professor? You'll understand there's no special treatment for anyone in this sort of investigation. Come with me, Josefa Horseman.'

DC Taleca, armed with a clipboard, led the other boys to the shade of trees bordering the field. Horseman wished he could go with them, then dismissed his nervousness as irrational. What could he possibly have to fear? All he had to do was tell this detective what had happened.

3

'Sit here.' DS Ratini pointed to the wooden benches behind the goal posts.

Horseman sat down, dazed. Seru, his mentor and captain, had taught him so much just by being the brilliant player he was. He sat at the officer's direction, shielding his eyes from the glaring sun with his hand.

'Sir, how could Seru die so suddenly? No one could be fitter or stronger.'

DS Ratini let out an exaggerated sigh. 'Look here, it's my job to ask the questions and yours to answer them. Understand?'

'*Io*, yes, sir. When I opened the shed door, I thought there was no one there.

Then, when I opened the shutters, I saw Seru slumped over in the corner. I thought he was asleep, but—

'Did you hear me? I ask the questions!'

'But I thought—'

DS Ratini leaned forward, jabbing his finger at Horseman. 'Don't think! Just answer! What is it with you USP students? You're supposed to be bright, but you can't follow a simple instruction, eh.'

'Sorry, sir.'

'What sort of a name's Horseman anyway? You look Fijian, but that's an English name.'

Horseman often enjoyed explaining the origin of his surname, but this was not one of those times. The short version, then. 'I have a European ancestor sir, who survived a shipwreck on Vanua Levu, along with a horse. He adopted the name Horseman, which has been passed down the generations.'

'Hmm, really?' Horseman wondered if DS Ratini would regard all his answers so sceptically.

'What are you studying here?'

'Business and Computer Studies, sir.'

'Hmm. Have you managed to pass? So far, that is.'

The detective's hostility was wearing Horseman down. Was that Ratini's purpose? If so, he was succeeding. Horseman expected questions about his discovery of Seru, but until now, Ratini had avoided the only topic that could possibly help them in their investigation. And more than anything, Horseman needed to know how his hero had died. Seru's family needed to know even more. His only choice was to cooperate with the hostile Ratini to get answers for them all.

'*Io*, I did pass my first semester, sir. I'm only in first year, but I hope I can keep on passing. My scholarship depends on it.'

'Scholarship eh? But you part-European families have plenty of money, don't you?'

Horseman knew the detective was baiting him, but he couldn't imagine why and he wouldn't rise. 'My father's a book keeper and my mother's a nurse, so we're lucky our income's regular. We get by comfortably enough, but we don't have plenty of money.'

Ratini shrugged. 'Lucky to be playing for USP 1st grade just out of school, aren't you?' His sneer implied Horseman's position in the team must be due to some trickery, or possibly bribery.

'*Io*, very lucky, sir. It's beyond my wildest dreams. Especially to have men like Seru and Coach encouraging me.'

Ratini again looked sceptical. 'Well, Josefa Horseman, tell me about what you did this afternoon. In detail.'

After Horseman had recounted the events, Ratini's mouth turned down in disapproval.

'So you're the team's dogsbody, Josefa. Is that right?'

Shocked by the man's rudeness, Horseman counted to five before replying. 'That's not how I look at it, sir. I'm the most junior team member, an apprentice I guess. I'm happy to carry out any jobs I'm given. I'm proud to be trusted.'

'And where's the kit bag you described?'

Finally, a fair point. Horseman had completely forgotten about his bag. He remembered carrying the water containers to the shed. Had he brought the bag as well? He shut his eyes, mentally retracing his steps. '*Io*, I carried the bag and water containers from the tap over there to the shed. I don't think I took them inside. All those things should be somewhere near the door.'

'Let's take a look then, shall we?' Ratini said.

Horseman trailed Ratini to the police tape in front of the shed. 'There it is, sir, just around the corner from the shed door. Maybe it was in the way and one of the police shifted it.'

'Seems to me you couldn't remember where you'd put it,' Ratini said with a smirk.

'True, but now it's come back to me. I did leave it beside the door.'

Ratini snorted. 'I'll take the bag. It's police evidence for now. You can go, but I'll be talking with you again. Got a phone number?'

'Just the dormitory public phone, sir. Let me write it down for you, my dorm and room number too.' Ratini glowered, then turned to a fresh page in his notebook and handed the book and a pen to Horseman. When Horseman handed it back, Ratini turned and ducked under the tape.

'Sir!' Horseman called out.

Ratini stopped, paused, then returned to the tape. 'What now?' he asked in an exasperated tone which was hard to understand since it was the detective who'd kept Horseman from his work, not the other way. Ratini was either perpetually irritated and grumpy, or something in Horseman had set him off.

'Sir, perhaps I could help by visiting Seru's family. Do you know whether they've been told of his death yet? His parents may well want to talk to me, since I found their son.'

Ratini drew his brows together to form one thick black line. He wagged his finger at Horseman once more. 'Just don't interfere in police business, boy! You think

we'd forget to inform the deceased's
family? The arrogance of you students!'
The detective turned again and headed for
the abandoned kit bag, shaking his head.

4

Seru might have lived if only he, Horseman, had arrived earlier for training. The thought nagged at him, but speculation about what might have been could rarely be settled one way or the other. He'd learned that in endless rugby post mortems. Beating himself up about it now could not help Seru.

But the Suva police were something else. His local police post on the island of Ovalau housed a few friendly constables in blue uniforms: one propping up the doorpost exchanging pleasantries with passing citizens, another typing laboriously on an old black typewriter and a couple in a back corner mellowing at the kava bowl. Although the officers came from other islands, the community welcomed their willing help when accidents, storms and fights threatened the sleepy villages. Sometimes a constable drove Horseman's mother, district nurse Sala Horseman, to deliver a stubborn baby or transported the ill to her clinic in the tiny town of Levuka. Homesickness washed through him just remembering the Ovalau constables.

Like everything else in Suva, the police were different here. Of course, Horseman had heard of detectives, but he'd never seen one before. Surely DS Ratini could not be typical. His casual dress, bad temper and undisguised hostility to Horseman were baffling. Forbidding Horseman to seek out Seru's family—why? His captain was a giant, or had been. Not only a talented and skilled player, an outstanding athlete, but a charismatic leader. All the USP teams followed Seru, aimed to emulate him, were devoted to him. Whatever Coach said, how could they survive his loss?

Horseman rubbed the tears from his cheeks. Rugby training usually lasted until six o'clock. He had to do something.

Maybe a punishing workout at the gym would help. He jogged in a beeline to the weatherboard and corrugated iron relic from World War 2. Here, on a rare piece of flat land, New Zealand officers had established the Fiji Defence Force compound. The remaining few rows of rectangular buildings now housed the Mathematics Department and the gym.

Catchy upbeat music blared through an open door. Twenty or so women bounded rhythmically to the shouted orders of their aerobics instructor. Horseman paused by the door, his eye caught by the bouncing red curls in the front row. Bindi! Only last week, turquoise streaks had animated her long black hair. Did she know about Seru? He must catch her after aerobics. As a close friend of Loa, Seru's girlfriend, Bindi needed to know.

He signed in to the free weights room and pumped iron beyond his previous limits for the next 30 minutes until he heard the music stop. He towelled off his sweat, returning to the hall just as Bindi emerged. He judged by her happy smile that she hadn't heard about Seru yet. Bindi Chopra was a first-year business student like Horseman. Originally she'd enrolled in Fiji School of Medicine and had studied there with Seru and Loa, his girlfriend, for four years.

'Joe, what a surprise! Shouldn't you be at rugby training? You'll be in Seru's bad books!' She wagged her finger at him, grinning. She must have registered his expression and her smile vanished. 'What's the matter?'

He didn't know what to say. 'Training's cancelled. It's about Seru. I arrived to set up but he'd got there first. I found him, Bindi. In the shed.'

'Spit it out, Joe. What do you mean?'

'He seemed to be asleep, but I couldn't wake him, so I thought he could be unconscious. I ran for Dr Koroi, but she couldn't help him. She said he was dead. I was too late.'

Her lips parted and she stared at him for a few moments. Then she reached up and grabbed his upper arms, shaking them ever so gently. 'Whatever's happened, it's not your fault, Joe. How could it be?'

'But if I'd arrived earlier, maybe he'd still be alive.' A sob caught in his throat, but he managed to swallow it back.

'Whenever he died, it's not your fault,' she repeated. 'Did Dr Koroi tell you anything else?'

Horseman took a couple of deep breaths, hoping they might still the quaver in his voice. 'No. The police and the ambulance arrived. She stayed in the shed with them for a while.'

She released his arms. 'Have you had anything to eat yet, Joe?'

Horseman shook his head, surprised at the very idea of food.

'Well, you need to. You've had a shock—a bereavement, too. I know you hero-worshipped Seru. And I always crave food after exercise. How about we go across the road to Hare Krishna?'

She patted his arm. He wanted more of her comforting, but he couldn't afford even the modest Hare Krishna prices until his next scholarship payment at the end of the month.

'*Vinaka*, Bindi. I should be working on our accounting assignment, so I'd better go to the student canteen and then to the library.'

'Don't be too proud to accept a cheap meal from a friend, Joe! You won't get any worthwhile work done in the library after what's happened. We both need something a bit better than the student canteen tonight. I'll be deeply offended if you knock me back!'

So he let her lead him out the front gates and across Laucala Bay Road to the little group of shops that made a living from the university students and staff.

The USP branch of the popular Hare Krishna curry shop was itself organised like a canteen. It was peak hour, and when Horseman and Bindi emerged from the production line, their battered trays crowded with stainless steel bowls of curries, dhal and sambals, there was not a table to be found. Bindi unleashed a torrent of pleading in rapid Hindi on the cashier. The cashier looked sympathetic and ushered them to a tiny table just behind the kitchen door.

The warm spicy smell and the cool air-conditioning urged him to wolf the food, but he managed to mind his manners in front of Bindi, this sophisticated woman five years his senior, who treated him as her friend.

After ten minutes, the creamy paneer and thick dhal suffused his system. Horseman felt calm. Calm enough to think, anyway. '*Vinaka*, Bindi. I'm grateful. Look, you studied medicine for four years. How could a fit sportsman like Seru just die suddenly?'

'My opinion isn't worth much, Joe. I failed my last year of med. But, for what it's worth, it could be a congenital heart condition, an acute infection, an embolism—that's a blood clot—, lots of things, really.'

'So it's not unusual?'

'Yes, it's unusual, but it does happen now and then. Dr Young, the hospital pathologist, has an excellent reputation. He'll find out why Seru died. But I know how you're feeling, Joe. It doesn't seem possible that Seru's dead.'

'What about Loa? I bet she doesn't know yet. I should go up to FSM campus and tell her. She'll be broken-hearted. You're her best friend, come with me.'

Bindi smiled in just the same way as his big sisters often did—indulgently. 'You're a sweet kid, Joe. And you're right, Loa must know.' She frowned. 'But didn't Professor Hau'ofa turn up at training this afternoon?'

'Sure, he talked to Dr Koroi and the detectives. Then he put off training until tomorrow.'

'Well, then, Prof will tell Loa as soon as he gets home. She moved into the staff flat behind his FSM house a while back.'

Horseman felt a bit foolish. Like the Prof, Loa was Tongan, so it was natural he would look out for her. 'No, I didn't know that. We could still go and keep her company, talk. It might help. Don't you think? She shouldn't be alone tonight.'

'She'll be in a heap, Joe. She's adored Seru since we both met him four years ago. It would be better if you waited until tomorrow before visiting. Let Loa cry her eyes out tonight. I can't go up to Tamavua now, but I'll ring her flat later and make sure she's okay. And the Prof will be there. How are you getting on with the accounting assignment, by the way?'

'I haven't actually made a start. Thought about it though.'

Bindi gasped in mock horror. 'Thinking doesn't count, Joe! Go to the library and find the references now. Borrow the books or photocopy what you need. You can count that as a start.'

'But you said I wouldn't get anything done tonight! You actually dragged me across the road to come and eat with you.'

'That was before I knew you hadn't even started on it. Go on. You'll feel better knowing you've got the essential references.' Bindi smiled, encouraging him.

Horseman felt deflated. It seemed no one needed his help or company. But Bindi knew what to do, so he'd follow her advice and visit Loa tomorrow. He headed for the library, doubtful he'd make much progress with his assignment tonight.

TUESDAY

5

The bus driver ground the gears as he changed down for the steep climb up Edinburgh Road. Horseman wondered if the old bus would make it. He glanced at the front pages of both papers he'd bought at the bus stop. No mention of Seru's death. He opened the *Fiji Times* and scanned each page until he came to the short article on page four.

Sudden death of USP 1st grade Captain

Seru Namata, aged 24, star of USP rugby, collapsed in the changing shed before training yesterday. He was pronounced dead by attending doctors,

*among them USP's celebrity coach,
Professor Lakepi Hau'ofa, who stated:
'Seru was an outstanding player and
captain who had a stellar future ahead
of him in international rugby. He was
also an excellent medical student who
looked forward to a career serving his
fellow Fijians. His death has shocked
all of us who knew him and left the team
in deep grief. However, USP teams will
try even harder to win without him, as
he would want.'*

*Son of Mareka and Vilisite of Kila
village, Central district, Seru attended
Kila primary school and Queen
Victoria School. The cause of Seru's
death is being investigated by the police.*

So, nothing new yet. Horseman turned
to *The Sun* and found the report on page
two under *Shock Rugby Death: Police
Investigate*. But beneath the sensational
headline there was no extra information.

He winced at the acrid smell of unburnt
diesel and looked out the glassless window.

The old bus had made it up to Samabula junction and was puffing at the traffic lights. When Horseman had first encountered the junction, he'd thought a fire must be raging close by, so strong was the burnt-rubber exhaust smell. Now he held his breath until the bus was through the junction, ascending even higher to the more salubrious suburbs and embassies along the ridge of Princes Road. Although the white-washed walls spilling bougainvillea and alamanda were attractive, the view beyond, the emerald ranges dropping to scalloped turquoise bays and glittering sea, brought tears to his eyes. The view reminded Horseman of his home island, Ovalau. Seru would never see this loveliness again. Perhaps heaven was more beautiful, but Horseman couldn't imagine how.

He was snatched from his reverie when the driver turned up the radio for the 12 o'clock news. The first items covered President Clinton's free trade deal with Canada and Mexico and the worsening drought in the western islands. Next came the news he'd been waiting for.

'More on the tragic death of promising rugby player Seru Namata, captain of USP first grade. Police are speaking to family and friends who may shed light on the cause of his death, which remains unknown.'

The newsreader made it sound like the police had suspicions about Seru's death. Could this possibly be true? He wondered if Seru's family and Loa knew about it. As the labouring bus was now only five minutes away from the FSM campus on Tamavua Heights, he reflected that Loa might already know more about Seru's death than he did.

6

'Follow this driveway, turn left, and Prof Hau'ofa's house is at the end of the street,' a student told Horseman.

The directions proved correct. He hurried to the detached flat at the back and called out from the porch. 'Are you there, Loa? It's me, Joe Horseman.' He waited but there was no answer, so he walked around to check for a back door. The word 'flat' was a misnomer. Each of the large houses for academic staff had a small, detached building behind or beside it. They were intended to house both a laundry and the domestic staff who used it. Horseman had been surprised to find that some USP lecturers rented out their staff flats to students, or employed students to clean their houses. He couldn't quite explain why, but he felt uncomfortable about this practice.

He looked across the garden to Coach's house. There was Loa, hanging washing on the line strung underneath the elevated house. He waited till she'd emptied her basket and turned back to her flat, then approached. Her wavy black hair hung loose around her drooping shoulders. She dragged her heels as if they were lead. She didn't seem to hear his first greeting.

'*Bula*, Loa. How are you?' Stupid question, he only had to look at her to see how she was. But he'd always been awkward around Seru's beautiful Tongan girlfriend. Around any girl really.

Taken aback, she recoiled before recognising him and relaxing. '*Bula*, Joe, how good of you to come to see me.' She lowered her eyes but gave him a small smile and her hand, which lay listless in his own for a second or two. She looked up at him.

Her red-rimmed eyes held his gaze. 'As you can see, Joe, I'm a bit of a mess.'

'Can…can I make you a cup of tea?' His banality disgusted him.

A tiny hint of amusement played at the corners of her mouth. 'That's so thoughtful, Joe. *Io*, a cup of tea would be nice, but I'll make it. Come in.'

The flat, unlike Coach's elevated house, was built on a concrete slab. Loa kicked off her flipflops on the little porch and Horseman removed his trainers, leaving them neatly beside a flourishing pot of basil. The words he wanted to say to Loa fled his mind.

The combined living room and kitchen was attractive, with floral curtains at the windows and bright-fringed pandanus mats on the floor. A battered cane sofa and coffee table faced a small television perched on an old-fashioned tea trolley. The small dining table overflowed with books, folders, loose photocopies and general student clutter.

'I'll get tea, Loa. You sit down and have a rest.'

'No, you don't know where anything is, let me.'

It was Horseman's turn to be amused. 'Let's not argue, I'm here to help. It's not exactly a big kitchen, is it? I've already spotted your teapot on the shelf above the sink.'

Loa shrugged and sank onto the sofa, which sagged beneath her. 'Okay. Everything you need is on the bench or the shelf above. No need to dive into my messy cupboards.'

Horseman raised his hand. 'I promise!' He caught his lighthearted tone and kicked himself for joking in the face of tragedy. But Loa gave him a weak smile in the same big-sisterly way that Bindi always did.

When he brought her tea, Horseman steeled himself to speak of Seru. 'I want to tell you what a wonderful guy Seru was to me—still is. He'll always be my hero. I was totally lost here when I arrived in February. My first time in a city, first time studying on my own. I only knew life on Ovalau and in a boys' boarding school. I felt like I didn't belong in a university, like a complete fraud.'

Loa nodded, her face serious. 'I did too, Joe. I think that's how most new students feel inside, but like you, I thought I was the only one. Imagine coming to Suva from tiny Tonga! At least you were in your own country.'

'*Io*, that's what my mum told me. And she always said to make each day better than the one before. Only I could do that, she would say. I loved rugby at school, so I screwed up my courage to turn up for the trials here. I hoped against hope that I might make the third grade team. I fumbled the ball a couple of times so I was sure I'd miss out.

'I couldn't believe it when Coach called my name out—just twelve of us to fill vacancies across all the grades. Seru congratulated me and shook my hand. "Now you're one of us, Joe, but you'll work hard for the privilege," he said. I assumed I'd made third grade, or even a reserve. After he told me I'd be joining him in first grade, I was speechless. He had a big grin on his face. "I warn you, I'm a slave driver and you're my youngest slave!"

' "Wow, I'll do anything, sir," I told him.

'Seru burst out laughing. "You may be my slave, but no need for *sir*. Call me Seru!" I knew then I belonged.'

Loa smiled again, tears welling.

'Seru spent a lot of time getting me up to scratch for the start of the season. Coach, too. Technique, tactics, fitness, teamwork. I owe them both a huge debt, but especially Seru. He was my captain, trainer and team mate, all in one.

Loa's tears overflowed now. 'And a slave driver?'

'I was a happy slave. He was brilliant. I can only dream of playing like him one day.'

'He told me you'd be a better player than him if you worked hard enough. I'm not sure if he was pleased about the prospect, but that's what he said.'

Horseman was astounded. Seru had only ever pointed out his deficiencies to him, which was what Horseman expected.

He felt his own tears welling now. He shook his head in disbelief and to cover his awkwardness, asked, 'Can I pour you more tea, Loa?'

'Yes, Joe, the tea has done me good. You have, too.'

When he returned with her tea, Loa was standing, tears now rolling down her face, her shoulders trembling. He put the mug down on the coffee table. She seized his arms, leaned her head against his chest and sobbed. As he lifted his arms to her shoulders, she pulled him close, holding on tight round his waist, binding herself to him. Tentatively, he patted her back, but it was only a moment before a sharp rap on the open door disturbed their shared grief.

'Detective Sergeant Ratini, Miss Tupou. Say goodbye to your visitor, if you please. I want to talk to you.' Ratini smirked as he suddenly recognised Horseman, who was dismayed by the conclusion the hostile cop would draw. He had to admit it was how he would interpret the scene himself.

'Aha, young Horseman eh? Just wanting

to help the bereaved again, are you? It's time you left.'

Horseman pulled back but Loa hung on to him. 'I'll talk to you, detective, but only if my friend can stay as a witness to protect me. I've heard police officers are not always to be trusted.' She looked up at Horseman, whose heart was battering his ribs in embarrassment as much as anger or fear. 'Please don't go, Joe.'

'As you wish, Miss Tupou. Sit down, please, both of you,' Ratini's tone was again sarcastic.

Loa straightened, flashed a haughty look at Ratini, then seated herself on the sofa with admirable aplomb. Horseman sat beside her and Ratini perched on a dining chair he drew up to face them.

'Constable, I need you to take notes,' he yelled. One of the officers Horseman remembered from the previous day entered, pulled up another dining chair for himself and produced a notebook and pen from his pocket.

'Cosy little housegirl's flat you've got,

Miss Tupou. Better than the student dormitory eh? How much rent do you pay Professor Hau'ofa for this?'

Horseman had to butt in. 'I must protest, Sergeant. How is this relevant to your investigation into Seru's death?'

'I decide what's relevant, Mr Horseman.' Ratini sounded amused yet insistent. Horseman decided he shouldn't rise to his bait any more.

Loa calmed herself and answered. 'I live here rent free in return for helping Mrs Hau'ofa with housework and the children. It suits us both.'

'How much time did the deceased spend here, eh?'

'Seru visited often, Sergeant. We used to study together. He also visited the Prof a lot to discuss rugby.'

'Ah yes, rugby. Quite the star, your boyfriend, eh?'

'Yes, Seru had a huge talent and he trained very hard.'

'And I guess your professor helped him get to that extra level, eh?'

Loa looked a bit puzzled. Horseman couldn't see where this was going either. 'I suppose so. He's a really good coach,' she said after a moment's pause.

'What drugs was the deceased using, Miss Tupou?'

'Drugs? What do you mean?'

'You're a medical student, you must be familiar with the word and its meaning, eh? I mean any kind of drugs in the form of pills, powders or liquids that he may have inhaled, injected or swallowed. Clear enough?'

Loa's mouth trembled. She pressed her lips together before replying. 'If he had a field injury, he might take anti-inflammatory ibuprofen or paracetamol, but I'm not aware of anything else.'

'Really? When you're so close? Like husband and wife, I hear.' Ratini's leer angered Horseman.

'Detective Sergeant, I must protest. Please treat Miss Tupou with respect. She is cooperating with you when she is suffering shock and grief. Such personal remarks are completely irrelevant and malicious.' Horseman was aghast at how pompous he sounded and knew Ratini would delight in making him suffer for it.

Ratini grinned in triumph. 'Why don't you get down off your high horse, sir! I don't need lessons from a kid like you. Sir.' He turned to Loa again, with an exaggerated bow. 'Miss Tupou, as I was saying, your long-term relationship with the deceased must have put pressure on him, I guess.'

Loa frowned. 'What do you mean?'

'Oh, you know, pressure to get married from parents and yourself, the stress of gossip about you two, the strain of losing his freedom as a bachelor, eh? All sorts of stresses and strains.'

Horseman seethed but restrained himself.

Loa straightened her back, held her head high and stared at Ratini with all the hauteur of a Tongan princess. 'I am not aware of any such pressure or stress, detective.'

'Really? A man could crack under four years of that sort of pressure, I reckon. I gather that's how long you've been his girlfriend.'

'If that's what you want to call me, yes. But Seru and I helped each other with any stress or pressure, Sergeant. We didn't add to it.'

'All that study, too. All those exams. All those rugby matches. Very, very stressful, especially as a man gets older.'

Horseman couldn't help butting in against his better judgement. 'Just what are you getting at, Sergeant? What did Seru die of? Have you got the post mortem results and you're not telling us? We need some straight information, not these rude insinuations!'

'You're a witness, Mr Horseman. You don't get any information that's not available to the general public.' He nodded at the newspapers on the coffee table. 'Keep your eyes and ears peeled and you'll find out along with everyone else.'

Horseman knew he'd asked for that put-down.

Ratini crossed to the windows, pulled a small radio from one of his pockets, mumbled into it and received a crackling response. Then he turned to his note-taker. 'Come on, Constable, let's be about our respectful enquiries. You'll see me again, Miss Tupou, thank you for your help. With your permission, my search team are waiting to look around this flat.'

'If you like, Detective Sergeant. Whatever you think necessary.'

Ratini nodded to Loa, ignored Horseman and left the flat.

Horseman had hoped to support Loa, but he had an inkling he'd just made things worse for her. He'd certainly made them worse for himself. In future he would avoid Ratini at any cost.

7

All the team made it to training at half past four, but their pace was subdued, kicks lacked vigour, ball handling was sloppy, tackles half-hearted.

Afterwards, Coach called them together. 'Boys, boys, all credit to you for turning up. However, your play was not up to standard. Understandably so. We face off against Police on Saturday. They're the top team this season, so far undefeated. But Seru's burning ambition was to win this game, to take Police down. Will you do that for Seru, boys? For your captain?'

The exhausted players, sides heaving, sweat and tears streaming, shifted their feet, uncomfortable. A few mumbled their agreement.

'Good! Training as usual on Thursday, half past four.'

Now it was Coach's turn to look uncomfortable; his gaze darted about his players as if seeking rescue. Fear prickled Horseman's skin.

Coach held up a hand and the team focused on him again. 'Boys, Detective Inspector Navala, the police officer in charge of Seru's case, got in touch with me not long ago. The pathologist has filed his preliminary post mortem report and I would prefer to tell you about it before you read it in the paper or hear it on the radio.'

The team greeted this with dead silence and full attention. Some players looked as alarmed as Horseman felt.

'I'll give it to you straight, boys. Dr Young found drugs in Seru's body. They were legitimate drugs prescribed for his rugby injuries but they were in high enough concentrations to contribute to his death. I want to stress that Dr Young hasn't yet reached a conclusion on the cause of Seru's death, because the results of a number of tests will take longer to come in. Nevertheless, the police think it probable that Seru killed himself. As he was a final year medical student, the police believe Seru would not accidentally overdose on his medicine, so they think suicide is the most likely explanation.'

What? Suicide? Every fibre of Horseman's being rebelled at the idea. Some boys froze, others shook their heads, shouted their protest, clutched their faces in their hands. The unified team was in disarray.

Coach raised his hand again. 'Boys, boys, remember that suicide is only what the police consider most likely at this moment. They may well change their minds when the pathology results are complete and as their investigation proceeds.

'What can we do, Coach?' Horseman called out.

'Win! Win on Saturday. And pray. I'm afraid I must go now.'

Professor Hau'ofa immediately strode away but Horseman chased after him. 'Coach, I know the police must be mistaken. I went to see Loa this afternoon and Sergeant Ratini barged in. He behaved objectionably to Loa. I wouldn't trust him at all. Can I talk to you?'

Coach stopped dead and stared at him. He looked at his watch. 'Look, Joe, I really do have to go back to FSM now, but I have a professorial board meeting here tomorrow at half past nine. I can see you at nine in the library.'

'I'll be there, Coach.' He would have to miss his accounting tutorial, but that didn't matter. His world had shifted. Now his studies would take a back seat. He had a new goal driving him and it wasn't to win Saturday's game.

8

'How could Seru do this to us? He's destroyed our team.'

'True. How can we win without him?'

'*Io*, and suicide is a sin. God will end our lives in His own time.'

'Come on, man. You've no right to judge. That's God's job too. Seru must have been suffering and we had no idea.'

'*Io*, we could have helped him.'

'But he had everything going for him! Top rugby player, top student, popular, about to become a doctor!'

'And his girlfriend's so gorgeous.'

'She's Tongan, you know, just like Coach. I heard she bossed Seru around.'

'Don't gossip, Maciu, it's not right.'

'Surely he died of a heart attack. Even if he did take too much medicine, that wouldn't kill him.'

'*Io*, Coach said the doctors haven't done all the tests yet. I bet the police will change their tune when the final report comes in.'

'Still, the police have to investigate. Seru's family and all of us need to know why he died.'

Horseman sat at the long student canteen table with eight of his team mates. Now they had something to argue about, their shock and grief was subsiding, or so it seemed. He hungrily dug in to his plate of dalo, the dense tuber that was Fijians' favourite staple. The kitchen hand had ladled on a generous serve of fish stewed with coconut and greens too.

Horseman generally refrained from spouting his opinion to his older, more experienced team mates, but now he wanted to speak, for Seru's sake and his own.

'We couldn't have had a better captain

and I, for one, couldn't have had a better mentor. To me, Seru was inspirational. I won't believe for a moment that he killed himself! He just wouldn't do that.'

A chorus of approval greeted Horseman's statement, surprising him. Maciu, another final year student, spoke again.

'Joe, you're a loyal kid and that's great. Especially as he treated you like a houseboy, ordering you about all the time.'

Horseman looked up, taken aback. 'No, I'm happy to help the team! I'm the apprentice, not the houseboy.'

'Fair enough, man,' Maciu replied. 'But you couldn't know everything about him. People have secrets. It's not impossible Seru committed suicide.'

Horseman nodded and ate some more dalo and fish. He had said enough. At least they'd listened and some of the boys agreed with him.

'*Bula*, boys!' Bindi came up to their table, carrying her tray. The boys started to shuffle their chairs along.

'Don't worry, boys, your table's full up.

I'd like to offer you my condolences. I know how important Seru was to all of you, and you to him.'

'*Vinaka vakalevu*, Bindi,' said Maciu.

'Finish your meal. I'll steal Joe from you though. Come and sit with me Joe.'

Some of the team shot curious looks at Horseman as he shrugged at them, picked up his tray and followed Bindi to a table close to the louvred windows overlooking the damp gully. He watched the exodus of hundreds of bats setting out to forage from the gully's two immense banyan trees. The last rays of the sun glinted off their fur.

'You're dreaming, Joe. Sit down and tell me how you are.' Bindi's red hair reminded him of the tawny bats' fur. Her round face was full of concern.

'I was just thinking Seru will never see the bats fly out at dusk again.'

Bindi nodded. 'I went to see Loa this afternoon and she told me about your visit. She said you were very gentlemanly in protesting to the detective about prying into her private business.'

'That Ratini! He's a bully. Poor Loa was in such a state about it. I had to do something to protect her from the bastard. Not that I succeeded. How was she when you saw her?'

'Oh, fragile, you know, but not too bad.'

As they ate, Horseman told Bindi more about Sergeant Ratini's interview—well, interrogation—with Loa.

Bindi's silver hoop earrings bounced as she set her tray aside and leaned towards Joe, her hands firmly planted on the table, her index fingers pointed at him. What was coming?

'Loa was touched by your visit today, she really was. But she's the last person who would want you to get offside with the police.'

'But I've done nothing wrong. What should I be worried about?'

'I can't say, but you did discover his body and…'

'And what? That was the worst moment of my life, Bindi. I'll never forget it. I just want to lie down and weep for Seru but that can't do him any good now.'

'Seru wouldn't want you to wallow in grief, I agree. You're right to want to do something, but antagonising the police isn't the way to go.' She was deadly serious. He wondered what exactly Loa had told her.

'I know I should accept the advice of my elders and betters. However...'

Bindi shrugged, throwing up her hands in mock despair.

Horseman smiled and continued. 'However, I must do something. I know I can't bring Seru back, but he still has his reputation, a very high one at that. That may be gone tomorrow with this talk of suicide, which I cannot accept. I want to save his reputation, so I must prove that he didn't kill himself.'

'I support your motive, Joe, but how will you do it?'

'I don't know yet, but first I have to find out more about him. I only met Seru six months ago and I guess I idolised him. He seemed to be everything I wished I could be. I know nobody's that perfect, so I need to talk to people who knew him better. Starting with you, Bindi.'

Bindi's eyes widened in dismay, but she soon smiled. 'Poor Seru, so much promise. Let me get some tea while I think.'

The brief tropical dusk was over, the only illumination was the campus lights and their reflection off the low clouds. When Bindi placed the steaming mugs on the table she was more relaxed.

'What was Seru really like?'

'Oh, handsome, charming, charismatic, but he knew he was all of those things, too. He could be kind.'

'Why did you say *could be* kind?'

'Because he often was. I shouldn't criticise the dead, but as you insist... People were usually happy to do whatever he wanted, just like you. They're so pleased to be associated with him and flatter him. He got used to that and naturally he loved the attention. But I have seen him put pressure on people who didn't want to follow his wishes. Mostly that brought them to heel.'

'How?'

'Oh, you know the Fijian ways, I'm sure, Joe. Constant teasing, which always appeared jokey, but wasn't. Funny public put-downs that all his crowd would laugh at. It goes on and on until the butt of all the jokes becomes like a scapegoat—a scapegoat that wants to rejoin the herd above all else.'

Horseman resisted Bindi's analysis of his hero. This was not the Seru he remembered.

'That sort of thing doesn't ring a bell with me. Who are these scapegoats?'

Bindi was quiet for a while, drinking her tea. 'I really can't recall individual cases.'

'What about drugs? Do you know what medicines he was taking?'

'I know nothing about that at all. He seemed fit and healthy, like all brilliant sportsmen. But if the drugs were prescribed, I can't see anything sinister going on.'

'*Vinaka*, I think that's all I can digest now. You're a good friend, Bindi.

'Everyone likes you, Joe. You're like

Seru in some ways, but nicer. Mind how you go. Strictly speaking, this is none of your business.'

WEDNESDAY

9

Horseman hurried to the library on the other side of the gully. The sudden squall dumped ten hours' worth of rain in ten minutes during breakfast and the gully's trickle was now a Class Four rapid scouring the earth. Grabbing the handrails, he swung onto the foot bridge. His feet slipped on the planks, slick with green algae plumped up by the rain. He landed on his backside, slid across the span of the bridge, hooked an arm round a post to stop himself shooting off the end onto the stone steps. He pulled himself to his feet, adjusted the bag still slung across his body, to be greeted by whoops from laughing students.

He grabbed an old towel from the boxes the staff put out at the library entrance during downpours. The towel took care of the drips, but Horseman's t-shirt and cargo pants were still wet. He shivered as he entered the air-conditioned library.

'You're Josefa Horseman?' an assistant asked. 'Professor Hau'ofa is waiting for you in Group Study Room 2.'

Not a good start. Coach rose to shake hands. He wore a white business shirt and striped tie with his formal grey sulu, the tailored wrap-around skirt worn by men throughout the South Pacific. A navy blue blazer hung over the back of his chair. It must be an important meeting he was going to.

Coach looked at Horseman intently as they shook hands. 'Let's sit, let's sit Joe. Tell me how you are now.'

A little alarmed that Coach was treating him as a patient, Horseman resolved to appear calm. '*Vinaka*, Coach, I'm okay. Seru is dead and we can't bring him back—that much has sunk in. What I can't accept is the police deciding that he killed himself. He would never do that, I know.'

'Joe, the police believe suicide's the most likely explanation, but they haven't decided anything yet. It's tragic, tragic, but not uncommon for young men to take their lives, you know.'

This was news to Horseman. 'Why?'

'Things get too much, they can't see any solution to their problems, they don't confide in anyone. To some, the only way out of intolerable stress and depression is to end it all.'

Horseman couldn't imagine himself on that path. 'But Seru! He had everything going for him. He was brilliant at everything. And so tough.'

'The toughest nuts can split easily if you tap them in the right place.' Coach mimed the action with his pen on the corner of the table. The horrifying image of Seru's head cracking open like a coconut startled Horseman.

This wasn't going anywhere. 'I don't understand about the drugs, Coach. Seru was fit. Can the pathology tests possibly be right?'

'Yes, yes, I'm confident they are. Dr Young's an excellent pathologist, thorough and persistent. We're lucky to have him, he could easily get a top appointment in Australia, but he stays in Suva because he married a Fijian lady who wants to bring up their children here.'

'But Seru often warned the team about alcohol and drugs. He was dead against them.' Too late, he recognised his gaffe and winced.

'Yes, yes, he knew the dangers first hand, you see. And he cared a lot about the team, especially fresh faces like you, Joe.'

'Do you know why he was taking these drugs?'

'Oh yes, I prescribed them.'

Horseman just stared at him, bewildered. Maybe he should walk away with his belief in Seru intact. Maybe Coach was covering up for something else with this crazy tale. No, he'd better hear Coach out.

'You see, when ambitious ruggers play hard from their teens to their mid-twenties, multiple injuries, none of them individually serious, stack up. Players like Seru persist through the pain because they don't want to let the team down and because they're ashamed of showing weakness. It's also a kind of warrior instinct that a lot of us share—Seru recognised it in you too, Joe.'

A stab of pride pierced Horseman, embarrassed though he was.

'Immediate pain from damage to muscles, tendons, cartilage and even bone can be effectively relieved these days with anti-inflammatory drugs. It's fine to take them if you're sore after training or a game. But there's a problem if you can't go on to the field without first dosing up. By masking the pain you're setting yourself up for serious injury that may require narcotic pain relief. Without careful medical supervision, injury, pain and drug use become a cycle, spiralling in one direction: downwards.'

'Surely Seru was too tough to get addicted to drugs?'

Professor Hau'ofa nodded slowly. 'Ah, toughness. Toughness is part of the problem, Joe. However, I can't discuss Seru's medical details with you, naturally, but I did prescribe, for sound medical reasons, the drugs identified by Dr Young in Seru's body. I've told him that.'

'*Io*, Coach, I didn't mean to…'

Coach looked at his watch. 'Before I go, I'd like to hear about your visit to Loa yesterday. She was rather disturbed by the interview with Detective Sergeant Ratini. What's your opinion?'

Coach paid close attention to Horseman's cautious summary, then glanced at his watch again. 'Joe, I want to impress upon you that physical injury is only one of the risks we take for rugby. The mental stress can be even worse. The pressure to perform at your peak, to win at all costs, comes from the team, coach, family and all the fans—from the whole country in internationals. For some of us, the pressure that's most irresistible comes from ourselves and I detect you're one of us. But no one can be the hero of every game. Remember that, Joe. Your long-term health must be your top priority.'

'*Vinaka*, Coach. I appreciate your advice.'

'Then take it, young man, take it. You're only subjecting yourself to more stress by challenging the police with your personal mission to clear Seru's name. We all must accept what has happened and honour Seru by winning Saturday's game. We're against Police, so you'll easily rustle up some killer instinct.'

'If DS Ratini's on the team, I'll have no trouble at all.'

Horseman stood as his coach put on his blazer. They shook hands, Coach looking into Horseman's eyes intently again. Then Professor Hau'ofa replaced his chair neatly under the table, picked up his umbrella and brief case, and made his exit.

Far from finding answers, Horseman was only more confused. He accepted everything the coach had said. If Seru had overdosed on prescription drugs to make

Saturday's game against Police, his death was an accident, not suicide. He still couldn't comprehend why Seru, so successful at everything, would want to end his life, nor why others could believe that he had done so.

10

Horseman eventually found the pathology department of the Suva Memorial Hospital. It was tucked away underneath at the back, accessed by a roller door bearing the sign *Deliveries*. That was one way of putting it, he supposed. Just along from the roller door he found a plain blue door with a buzzer marked *Reception*. He buzzed and the door clicked. He entered a narrow white hall that led to a waiting room. He sneezed at the sharp antiseptic smell. A very young Indian man in a white coat and a white shower cap stood beside the tiny reception counter.

'How can I help you, sir?' he asked.

Horseman smiled. '*Bula*. I need to see

Dr Young, please. If he's not free I can wait.'

'In relation to which case, sir?'

'Seru Namata, Doctor.'

'Oh, thank you, but I am not being a doctor, sir. I am Shoban, laboratory technician assisting Dr Young.' Shoban smiled. He could not have been more than Horseman's own age. 'Please be taking a seat while I locate Dr Young.'

When the door opened again Horseman recognised the lanky blond man who had come to the campus rugby field with the police on Monday. He looked sympathetic as he shook Horseman's hand.

'Hello there. Dr Matthew Young, pathologist. My condolences on Seru's death. What a dreadful loss you've suffered.'

Horseman introduced himself.

'Are you Seru's younger brother?' Dr Young asked.

'No, doctor. I'm on his team.' He felt the doctor sizing him up.

'Are you the player who discovered Seru in the shed?'

'Yes, sir.'

'Hmm, that must have been a great shock. If you've come to tell me something you've since remembered, I'm not the right person, I'm afraid. You need to tell the police.'

'No, I've told them everything. I've come because you'll be able to answer my questions.'

Dr Young smiled. 'Okay, ask away.'

'What were the drugs found in Seru's body? Were they all prescribed for him by Professor Hau'ofa?'

'Hang on a minute, mate. I've spoken about this to the Prof, who's a valued colleague of mine. He did know Seru was taking the drugs we identified, as and when needed. But you know, the analysis is not yet complete, and until I've finalised my PM report, I can't give you those answers.'

Horseman tried not to let his disappointment show. 'Were the concentrations of the drugs you found enough to kill Seru? He was so young and strong.'

'Okay, just speaking generally, forensic

analysis is not an exact science. Rather, the analysis is exact, but the conclusions we draw can't always be exact. As you suggest, the same dose of a toxic substance may kill one person and not another, in some circumstances and not in others. There are even more ifs and buts when a combination of toxins is involved. The total effect may be more or less than the sum of each drug acting alone.'

'We both know that something killed Seru, doctor. If it wasn't the drugs, what other possibilities are there?'

'Good question, mate. So far, I haven't found any cause apart from the effects of drugs. But that doesn't mean there isn't one, not by a long shot. And you know, not all drugs leave traces in the body.'

'You see, doctor, Professor Hau'ofa told us the police believe Seru may have committed suicide. I just can't believe that. No way.' Dr Young looked sympathetic again.

'So, my only course is to prove he didn't kill himself. And I can't do that without finding out more, asking experts like yourself questions.'

'Josefa, your loyalty does you credit. But the answers you find might not be the ones you're looking for.'

Horseman didn't understand what Dr Young was driving at. 'What I want is the truth.'

'Do you? Not everyone does, you know.'

Horseman was still confused. 'Please, doctor, don't give up. Can you check everything again, please? Seru's reputation is at stake.'

The pathologist smiled. 'Sure I will. And the outstanding results should be in today or tomorrow—they may shed some light.'

'*Vinaka vakalevu*, doctor.'

'By the way, it wasn't me who suggested suicide to the police, you know. I understand there's some other evidence that's pointing them in that direction. You'll have to ask them. All the best to you, mate.'

11

At all costs, he must avoid DS Ratini, not only because the sergeant would never divulge any information to Horseman, but also because he hated the man and hate was an emotion Horseman rarely felt and found disturbing.

He waited near a public phone in the shade across the street from the station entrance. It was half past one and officers were returning from lunch. When the phone box was at last vacant, Horseman called the station and asked to speak to DS Ratini. He hung up when the receptionist offered to transfer him. He repeated his call twice more at ten-minute intervals, with the same result. But when he made his fourth call and was told DS Ratini was no longer available, he asked to speak to Detective Inspector Navala about the Seru Namata case. To his surprise, after a few moments' delay, the receptionist replied the DI would see him right away.

***

Detective Inspector Navala was curious about the young student who entered his office. His name identified him as one of the numerous descendants of the famous survivor of the wrecked ship that brought the first horse to Fiji in the early nineteenth century. That ancestor's true name had been lost, but his equestrian skills had saved him from the ovens and won him favour with the chief, who desired the horse above all else.

Few European genes were apparent in young Josefa, except perhaps for the slightly lighter brown skin and more loosely crinkled hair which, to any Fijian who didn't know his name, would place him in the Polynesian-influenced eastern islands. His face was pleasantly open, his eyes intelligent, his medium height and solid build ideal for rugby, his greeting courteous, his handshake firm.

'*Bula*, pleased to meet you, Josefa Horseman. One of my cousins married Elisa Horseman, who must surely be your relative.'

'*Io*, sir. I think she's a distant cousin of my father.'

'So, we are connected. Like most Fijians. Take a seat and tell me why you've come to see me.'

Horseman looked straight at DI Navala. From the moment he entered, young Horseman's seriousness was impressive. No bashful grins or nervous laughs that were typical of boys in men's bodies. DI Navala judged this boy to be on a mission.

'Sir, as you know, I found my captain Seru Namata collapsed in the USP rugby shed on Monday. I didn't know if he was alive or dead, so I ran to our campus clinic for a doctor. Yesterday, our coach,

Professor Hau'ofa, told us about the preliminary post mortem results. He said the police considered Seru most likely committed suicide.'

'*Io*, at this stage it does seem likely, Josefa. We'll know more when Dr Young finishes his investigation. Certainly, suicide can't yet be ruled out.'

Horseman frowned. 'But I can rule it out, sir. Without doubt. You see, I knew Seru well. He picked me for his first grade team and kind of adopted me. He was dedicated to the team, his studies…he'd be a doctor in another year. There's no way he would kill himself. It's impossible.' The boy shook his head vehemently.

'So I want to prove that. I'm speaking to people who can give me more information. I've come to you because Dr Young told me today that you've found some evidence pointing to suicide. Not the drugs he found in Seru's body, but something else. He wouldn't say what it is. He advised me to ask you.'

This youngster was loyal, passionate and

brave. He could prove to be persistent, too. Time would tell. DI Navala decided to test Horseman's mettle with the evidence.

'Well, I trust we can rely on your discretion just as we can rely on Dr Young's?'

'*Io*, sir.' Horseman's face was earnest.

'Let's see what you make of what we found in Seru's room, then. Your hero was quite organised, kept a diary, mostly just listing his commitments for each day. However, he sometimes wrote comments. It's often not clear what or who is the subject of his thoughts. This is the comment he wrote two weeks ago. "I can't go on with this, it's impossible". This note, together with the positive drug traces, is why we think Seru may well have ended his own life.'

DI Navala leaned back in his chair, steepling his fingers in front of his crisp striped business shirt as he waited for Horseman to respond. The boy was visibly shaken. Would he accept or challenge the evidence?

After what seemed like an age, Horseman asked, 'Sir, why do you think Seru's note means he intended to kill himself? Sure, that's possible, but there are alternative interpretations too. It could be about his uni assignments, or the strict physical training he set himself, or maybe the doses of drugs he was taking for pain… even some pressure his girlfriend was putting on him. Most likely, all these things together were too much, but he was thinking of going easier on some of them, maybe giving up one or two, but certainly not of giving up on life, of killing himself!'

So, young Horseman was a challenger. DI Navala had guessed as much. He wondered why Horseman had mentioned his hero's girlfriend. Perhaps he knew more than he was admitting. Ratini had mentioned Horseman was visiting Loa Tupou when he'd gone to FSM yesterday to question her. He scribbled a reminder in his notebook. 'What you've just said is logical and plausible in theory, Josefa. What years of practice tell me is first, that suicides very often leave a written message about their intention and second, that the most likely to commit suicide are ambitious and able young men. Their friends and family think they're successful and happy, with bright futures ahead. Sadly, this is often not true, not true at all. Take my advice, Josefa. Don't be overly ambitious.'

'No, sir. At least, I'm not ambitious for myself—I don't think so, anyway. But I am keen to clear Seru's name, to prove he didn't put an end to his own life. I just know he didn't do that, in spite of what you say about others. You didn't know him, sir.' The boy's lip was trembling. It was time to end this interview.

'*Vinaka* for coming in, Josefa. It's a tribute to Seru that he has such loyal friends. I will consider all your helpful suggestions to explain the note in Seru's diary. Please don't hesitate to get in touch if any other relevant information comes your way.'

DI Navala handed Horseman one of his cards and shook hands. Horseman certainly had the brains for university study. How his teachers would cope with his challenging nature he couldn't say, never having gone near a university himself.

12

Horseman stopped his weights session in time to meet Bindi at the end of her circuit training class at six o'clock.

'Hey Joe, how's it going?' Flushed from exercise, her face looked almost cheerful again.

'Pretty busy today, Bindi.'

'Does that mean you didn't take my advice then?' Her tone was playful.

Horseman shrugged. 'Not exactly. I did approach the police because I owe it to Seru. Got time for a chat about it?'

'I'm meeting a friend in town so I can't stop for long. Let's get chai here.'

They went out to the insect-screened

gym verandah. Bindi secured a couple of plastic chairs while Horseman ordered at the counter. Until this year he'd never heard of chai, never known that the handful of Indian families in Levuka drank a different kind of tea.

'I hate these mouldy chairs,' Bindi said when he returned with two giant mugs of chai. 'If mould can grow on glossy white plastic, what hope do mere creatures of flesh and blood have? We must host masses of it.'

'Maybe the chai's an antidote. Drink up!' Horseman said. While Bindi sipped, he related the gist of his meeting with DI Navala.

As Horseman spoke, her brows drew together in a frown. 'I did warn you not to poke your nose into police matters,' she said in a low voice.

'You understand why I need to—I know you do.' Horseman now swigged his cooling chai. 'There's so much I don't know. I don't even know how you met Seru.'

'Loa and I met along with all the other first-year Med students at Orientation. Loa was shy and homesick, just like many of us. She and I teamed up pretty soon. Seru was in second year and just like he is now—was, I mean. He stood out from the crowd in all ways. Loa picked him long before he noticed her, even though she's so beautiful—those huge eyes and fair skin! It surprised me how determined she was to get him. She kept on turning up to rugby games, even took up kayaking because he was into it—and she was patient. Over the long summer break, she returned to Tonga and Seru found he missed her. Men! They started dating at the beginning of second year. The rest, as they say…'

'So, the course of true love was smooth after all? Until now, of course?'

Bindi smiled. 'It seemed to be—no dramatic bust-ups anyway. I suppose I mainly know about all this from Loa's point of view. Seru never once confided in me about her. I wouldn't expect him to, either.'

'Had anything changed between them

recently, do you think?'

'Funny you should ask that. I have noticed a bit of a change in Loa this year. Hard to put my finger on it, though. She doesn't talk about him so much any more. When I've asked her about him lately, she might just say he's okay, but nothing more. Actually, she's been quite tight-lipped now I think about it.'

'When did that start, do you remember?'

'Hmm, probably since she moved to the Prof's flat at the beginning of first semester.'

'Don't you think that's a bit odd, Loa living in his maid's flat?'

Bindi shrugged. 'It's common enough on campus—here and FSM too. Don't go reading too much into that situation.'

Horseman looked at Bindi, bewildered. What sort of interpretation was he suspected of?

'I've got to dash, Joe. My advice to you remains the same. I have your best interests at heart, you know.'

It had never occurred to him to doubt it.

Now, her insistence made him wonder if it were true. Maybe there was another reason Bindi wanted him to drop his pursuit of the truth about Seru.

'I'll walk with you to the bus stop,' he said.

THURSDAY

13

'Why does DS Ratini want to see me?'
Horseman asked the driver, Constable
Nikhil Maharaj.

'Don't ask me. DS Ratini didn't tell me.
He ordered me to find you on campus and
bring you to the station. Barring accidents,
I'll be getting this job done with no trouble.'
The constable turned to Horseman and
grinned.

'It must be about the death of Seru
Namata. I discovered his body. Are you on
that case?'

'Me? Oh, no. I'm just a car pool driver.'
He seemed happy with his allocated role.

'Still, in the car pool you'd hear a lot

about the investigations from the other drivers, wouldn't you?'

Constable Maharaj wagged his head from side to side, smiling. 'Sometimes.'

'Heard anything about Seru?'

'He's the USP rugby captain isn't it? Great player—so tough and fast. I've been seeing him several times, whenever Police are playing USP. Such a terrible thing, his death.' Constable Maharaj took his eyes off the road and turned to Horseman. 'My condolences. Was he your friend?'

'Yes, and my captain. I play for USP too. What does the car pool say about his death?'

'You know I shouldn't be saying anything, sir.' Constable Maharaj sounded official, but gave Horseman a friendly grin before slamming on the brakes as an old woman bearing a huge bunch of bananas on her shoulders scurried across the road.

'But?' Horseman prompted when his heartbeat returned to normal.

'But honestly, sir, the drivers are not knowing anything about this case.'

'I guess I'll find out why I'm here soon enough.' Horseman sighed and let Constable Maharaj concentrate on navigating the chaos of Suva traffic.

***

Constable Maharaj ducked his head at Horseman in apology as he ushered him into the dingy interview room where Detective Sergeant Ratini was pacing. Ratini's jeans were stained around the pockets and his tee-shirt was crumpled. The detective ignored Horseman's proffered hand. Despite his vow to stay calm, the discourtesy riled Horseman. Clearly, Ratini intended to provoke him but he mustn't let the bullying officer succeed. He sat on the chair Ratini pointed to. He even managed a polite smile.

'*Vinaka* for arranging the lift, sir. How can I help you?'

'As you're taking such an interest in my investigation, *Mister* Horseman, I should tell you about a new lead that has emerged.' A mean smirk twisted the detective's mouth.

'Oh, that's good news, sir.'

Ratini shrugged. 'Maybe, maybe not. It depends who you are.'

Horseman could do nothing but wait.

Eventually Ratini came out with it. 'This morning Dr Young reported the latest lab test results. He's still not able to finalise the PM report, but it's looking like you were right. Your hero may not have committed suicide.'

Relief flooded through Horseman. He couldn't help smiling broadly at Ratini. 'That's wonderful, sir. I knew Seru could never do that.'

'Oh you did, did you? Man, between you knowing and me believing, there's a small matter of evidence.'

'*Io*, sir. What is the evidence?'

'With your vast experience as a detective, Mr Horseman, you'll appreciate the new evidence is confidential. However, we're now considering the possibility that your captain was murdered.'

'Murdered—Seru! But how? Who?'

Ratini nodded slowly. 'No flies on you,

are there, Mr Horseman? These are exactly the questions we're asking ourselves. And I think you might be able to help us.'

Horseman, bewildered, shook his head. 'Sorry, I can't take this in. No one would want to murder a man like Seru!'

'Oh, you'd be surprised, boy, you'd be surprised what some murderers tell us about their whys and wherefores.'

'I mean, do you suspect anyone?'

'Oh, as a matter of fact I have an idea. Classic textbook, really.'

Horseman was irritated with Ratini's toying.

'Sir, that means nothing to me, but if you can explain what you mean, I'm eager to hear about it.'

'Good! Well, statistics show that the person who *finds* the corpse and reports the victim's death is always a suspect and often turns out to be the murderer.'

'What? You're joking!'

'Not at all.'

'You mean I'm suspected of killing Seru? I worshipped him.'

'Aha, you're extremely emotional, aren't you, Mr Horseman? Love turns to hate so often in your personality type.'

Surely this was some sadistic game Ratini was playing. It couldn't have anything to do with the reality of the investigation. Should he just laugh it off and walk out? He had the feeling Ratini would love it if he did walk out. So no, he'd better stay, act like he took Ratini seriously and find out as much as he could.

'But why, sir? What motive could I possibly have?'

'Here's what I think, Mr Horseman. First, you worshipped Seru but he treated you like a dog. From what I've heard, he dumped on you all the jobs nobody on a rugby team wants to do. He bullied you, never let up on the teasing.'

'No, it wasn't like that at all!'

Ratini sneered. 'Second, you fancy his very attractive girlfriend, never mind she's years older than you. What hope could a boy like you have against Seru? While he's alive, that is. But, with him dead, you can charge in on your white horse to comfort the weeping beauty, true to your name. Even you might stand a chance if you play it right.'

Horseman was dumbfounded. 'This is crazy! None of this is true! Have you any evidence at all against me?'

'Sure, you were in the right place at the right time. You were alone at the field with Seru for some time before any of the others arrived for practice. Isn't that a fact?'

'That's true, but hardly proof.'

'I agree, Mr Horseman, but we're hounds with our noses on your trail. If you've nothing more to tell me, you're free to leave me to get on with the case.'

Horseman stood, his fists clenched against his thighs, fearing that, unrestrained, they might fly towards Ratini's jaw. 'Sir, I did not kill Seru, the idea is completely untrue. If anyone has told you I did, I suggest you turn your investigation in his direction, because he's lying.'

'Ah, we look in all directions, Mr Horseman. But I'll be looking in yours long and hard.'

14

His feet pounded the path around the harbour foreshore, as if he could restore order to his mind through the regular beat of his paces. But Horseman had no choice—he had to move. His axis had been jolted off-kilter by the revelation that Seru had been murdered. Not only that, but he was the chief suspect!

Was Ratini mad? Possibly. Sane or insane, the detective was a nasty piece of work, Horseman could see that. Maybe he was bluffing, just for the pleasure of feeling his victim squirming under his boot. Even if this was the case, which Horseman thought likely—hell, the alternative was terrifying—it would be reckless to ignore Ratini's threats.

He crashed into the chain-link barrier at the cargo wharf. His body running with sweat, knees quivering, he slumped against the springy fence. He must have started sprinting without knowing, lost in his thoughts. Take control!

He resumed jogging, but at an easier pace now, back along the path towards Ratu Sukuna Park and the stop for the USP buses. He couldn't let himself be Ratini's prey or plaything. He had to seize the ball himself and run with it, dodging the detective where possible, tackling him as a last resort. If Seru had been murdered, the only way Horseman could prove his innocence was to find the killer himself. He felt his legs speeding up and deliberately slowed his pace again, forcing his gaze to take in his surroundings. The sea glittered with oily rainbows as the sun pierced the grey clouds. The southeasterly trade breeze sprang up, cooling his body and swaying the palms beside the path.

How could he begin to look for Seru's murderer? His captain always said nothing was impossible, urging the boys to greater efforts with a grin on his face, ignoring their pleas for a break. As the shaft of sun moved ahead of him, Horseman understood that Seru would not let him give up.

After all, Seru did not die by a random act of violence. If drugs were the murder weapon, his killer was probably someone close to Seru, and quite possibly someone Horseman knew, too. That thought stopped him dead in his tracks, but if he tried to dodge the idea he'd never succeed. He controlled his panting, took a few deep breaths and crossed the raintree-shaded park to the bus stop.

***

Horseman had liked Dr Young when he first visited the hospital pathology department, so he now entered with some confidence. As the reception counter was deserted, he pressed the bell and waited. He was pondering whether or not he should tell the pathologist about Ratini's accusation when the door to the labs opened and Dr Young himself appeared. His white lab coat hung open over his green surgeon's scrubs.

'Hello, Joe. What can I do for you, mate?' Dr Young held out his hand.

Horseman shook hands with vigour, grateful for the friendly gesture. '*Bula*, Doctor. I'm hoping you can tell me a bit more about Seru's case. DS Ratini told me you have more test results now.'

Dr Young frowned. 'Well, come on in. I'm not sure you'll be satisfied with what I can tell you, but we can have a chat.'

The pathologist led the way into the lab. Benches covered with scientific apparatus lined three walls, while two parallel benches occupied the central space. White-coated assistants frowned at test tubes and made notes. Dr Young pointed to a door on the left.

'Take a pew in my office while I fill the kettle. You look like you could do with a cup of tea. Milk and sugar?'

'Yes to both, thank you.'

Like the lab, Dr Young's office was meticulously organised. Horseman looked out the window louvres to a view over the trees to the rusty rooftops fringing Suva Bay.

'There you go, mate. Sit down and get this inside you. You'll feel better. What've you been up to?'

Horseman took the large white mug and sat. 'I've been talking to DS Ratini down at the police station. He told me you had more test results now and you think Seru was murdered.' To hide his emotion, Horseman took a large gulp of scalding tea. He fought the reflex to spit it out, burning his throat as he forced himself to swallow it.

'Oops, too hot is it? Sorry.' Dr Young poured Horseman a glass of water. 'Drink all of this, it will reduce the burn.'

He felt like a total idiot, but he downed the glass of water, then another. 'Excuse me, Dr Young. Can you confirm what DS Ratini's told me?'

The grey eyes looked at him steadily.

'It's looking like murder now, yes.'

'How was Seru killed?'

'Look, Joe, I'm sure you understand by now that our test results are not public documents. Nothing can be made public until I've written my conclusions when all the data is in. That's not the case yet.'

'I do understand that, but I really need help here. I mean you haven't found at this late stage that Seru was shot or stabbed or drowned—you'd have known that right away. Could I be right in supposing that you must have discovered some additional poison or drug?'

Dr Young's sandy eyebrows lifted in surprise. 'You could, yes. I'm not saying you are, remember.'

'If I am right, how could the newfound poisons or drugs tell you it was murder rather than suicide?'

'That would be because the substances could be lethal and would never have been prescribed for Seru.'

Horseman agonised about divulging that Ratini had cast him as the chief murder suspect. If he told Dr Young this, it could seriously backfire and the pathologist might refuse to say another word. But if Dr Young dismissed Ratini's suspicion, the sympathy he'd already shown to Horseman might increase. He would have to take a gamble.

'Doctor, DS Ratini suspects I'm Seru's murderer. I swore I had nothing to do with Seru's death, but I don't think I changed his mind. You see, yesterday I was fighting to save Seru's reputation but today I'm fighting to save my own skin.'

The doctor's grey eyes were intense. 'That doesn't make sense to me. I can see you're a loyal mate, sticking up for Seru like you are. I wouldn't lose sleep over Detective Sergeant Ratini's accusations.'

He picked up a print-out from his in-tray. 'I can't tell you what's in this. Excuse me for a minute while I check up on the guys in the lab, will you, mate? Won't be long.' He winked at Horseman and returned the print-out to the top of his tray.

15

'Good work, boys, good work. That was an improvement on Tuesday's training. Seru will be smiling on us. Take a break tomorrow and we'll meet here an hour before the game on Saturday. Joe, don't forget to collect all the gear and bring it here good and early. Seru can't nag at you now, eh.'

'Got it, Coach. I won't forget.' Horseman wondered again why people regarded his jobs as an imposition. He enjoyed being useful. But he must talk to Coach about today's disaster.

'Coach, I badly need your advice if you have a few minutes.' Professor Hau'ofa frowned. Close up, he did look tired: the lines running from his nose to his mouth looked deeper, as did the furrows in his brow.

'Sure, Joe. Collect your things and walk with me to the car.'

'I've got the lot already.' Horseman slung two large sportsbags over his shoulders. He briefly relayed DS Ratini's two shockers.

'No, I don't believe Seru was murdered!' Coach thundered. The police are simply wrong. Sorry, Joe, but everything so far fits with suicide. And as for suspecting you, DS Ratini can't be serious! If he is, he's incompetent, malicious, or both. Probably both!'

'That's a huge relief to me, Coach. Your support means a lot. I was beginning to think the world was against me.'

'You're a good lad, Joe. Seru laid it on you a bit thick at times, but you took his teasing with good humour. We all respect you for it. Like you, too.'

'But I've got to take DS Ratini's

suspicion seriously, Coach. I went to the pathology department but Dr Young wouldn't tell me about the new results. However, while he was out of his office, I jotted down the substances identified in the latest report. I haven't had time to look them up yet, but of course, you'll know exactly what the implications are.'

Professor Hau'ofa stopped and turned to face him, a surprised smile on his face. 'Really, Joe, I'd never have thought it of you! You've got a list?'

'Coach, I've been accused of murder! I can only fight that with evidence!'

'No, no, Joe. I admire your resourcefulness. You pinched the lab report! Can I have a look?'

Horseman handed over the list. Professor Hau'ofa read aloud. 'Ibuprofen, paracetamol, codeine, fentanyl, insulin.

'Oh Seru! You knew better than to take all those in the same week! I see there's only a trace of fentanyl, not enough to do damage, but I suppose in combination... I prescribed that last year when he had a cartilage tear in his knee. He must have kept what he didn't need for a rainy day. He's not the only medical student to follow that practice, sadly. But insulin?' He shot a confused look at Horseman. 'Insulin? I can't think of any explanation for that.'

'What should I do about this?'

Coach said nothing more until they reached his car. 'Don't worry, Joe. I can't see Inspector Navala seriously considering you as a murder suspect. The PM report isn't finalised yet. Let's wait and see what Dr Young concludes. He'll share it with me as soon as it's done. Your dedication to Seru is admirable, but drop your probing now. It's only irritating the police. I need you to help defeat them on the field on Saturday. Here, let me give you a lift back to campus with those bags. You look wrung out.'

Horseman wasn't at all sure he should rely on Coach's advice, but he was grateful for the ride.

16

'So you see, Bindi, today hasn't been a good one. Honestly, it's been the worst day of my life.' Horseman looked across the library table at his friend. When he'd glimpsed her red curly head at the top of the stairs, he knew she'd help and he dashed to catch up. He must look desperate, because Bindi had glanced at his face, grabbed his arm and steered him to an empty group study room where they could talk. It was Horseman who spoke first, blurting out happenings, his thoughts and, although embarrassed to recognise this midstream, his feelings too. Bindi listened.

When he ran out of words, he rubbed

his hands over his face, hard. He couldn't remember what he'd just told her. Doubtful, he looked into warm brown eyes that reflected his own pain and confusion. He'd been expecting wise counsel from someone uninvolved.

'Man, this is unbelievable. How could the police put you through this? There's got to be something behind it we don't know about.'

'I've been thinking that, too. But where does that get me?'

'Look, Joe, when you asked me about Loa and Seru yesterday, I didn't tell you everything. I couldn't, because Loa's my closest friend. But now, with you under suspicion of murder, I must spell out the full story on condition that you pass it on to no one but the police, and only if you think it might save you.'

Horseman leaned towards her, desperate. 'I promise, Bindi. I have to know.'

Bindi ran a hand through her hair, looked down at the table top. 'I'm breaking a confidence here, so I'll cut it short—you don't need any explanations, just the facts. When Mrs Hau'ofa decided to stay in Tonga this year, Loa moved into their maid's flat in return for housework. Dormitories pall after five years, I can tell you, so it seemed a good arrangement. But before too long, Loa was sharing the Prof's bed as well as making it—don't ask me how and when because I don't know. I don't know if Seru knew from the beginning or how he found out but, as you can imagine, the situation has had a huge impact on him and Loa. I mean, they'd been a couple for years—everyone assumed they'd marry the moment they graduated. Loa told me about it months ago because she wanted to be honest with me, but she's said nothing since. When you told me the police thought Seru had killed himself, I could well believe it, because how could he have handled the triangle between the man who was his teacher, mentor and coach, the love of his life and himself?' She looked at him directly now, her eyes troubled.

Horseman could feel his own eyes

widening as she spoke, reacting like a child. He had to admit he was a child—no, a newborn—in this world of tangled triangles Bindi presented to him. Although he couldn't see how anyone might get into such a situation, he could easily imagine the destructive forces unleashed.

'Did, er, was Loa forced, do you think?' He couldn't bring himself to refer to Professor Hau'ofa right now.

'I don't know and I don't want to discuss possibilities. That would be nothing more than just gossip and that's something I don't do. She's my best friend. She told me it was complicated and she was handling it. Now you understand why she's been so withdrawn this year.'

'My guess is the Prof coerced her—Loa can't have had any choice or she wouldn't have done this. But it's obvious who fits the frame for Seru's murderer now. Isn't it?'

Bindi shook her head. 'Joe, I knew you'd react this way, but you've got to defend yourself—that's the most urgent priority. Please think carefully. I'd still advise you to keep well away from all this, if you can.'

'I can't. You know that. However, I'll let it sink in overnight and decide what to do in the morning. I've still got to get the bare essentials of my accounting assignment done before the library closes. That's due tomorrow, too.'

'Best of luck, Joe. Look, I'll have to let Loa know about our conversation. I'll phone her at home. It's not going to be easy, but I owe her that.'

'Please give her my best. Perhaps I could drop in to see her tomorrow afternoon.'

Bindi smiled. 'Don't just drop in, Joe. She's grieving, she needs a bit of space.'

Joe nodded, disappointed. 'Sure. Sorry.'

'I've just had a better idea. Loa will be in clinical classes at the hospital tomorrow until five o'clock. She's so flat out these days I often meet her in the canteen there on a Friday to catch up. Why don't you join us? She'll know what I've told you by then and it'll be less awkward for all of us.'

Joe was overwhelmed at Bindi's thoughtfulness. 'That's kind of you, Bindi.

A good idea, too. By then I'll have made my decision and Loa has a right to know that, too. I'll see you tomorrow, then.'

'Take, care, Joe.' Bindi patted him on the back and left.

Horseman walked along the rows of shelves to the carrel where he'd been working before Bindi came in. The thick medical reference book was still on the desk, his notepad beside it and his bag on the floor. He didn't know why he hadn't shared his research with Bindi. When he'd been about to tell her about the list of drugs, something made him hesitate, and the right moment passed.

FRIDAY

17

Mid-afternoon and Horseman was still hovering near the police station's public counter. DI Navala would see him when he was free, so the officer said. After a sleepless night tormenting himself with the rights and wrongs of dropping Bindi's bombshell on the police, he was still in two minds. He knew Loa would hate him for it and rightly so. But Bindi was correct; he must save his own neck because nobody else would or could. As for Coach— Horseman now despised the man who only yesterday was his respected mentor. Still, the wait was eating away at his resolve. Maybe he should just walk out now. He strode through the stairwell, his eyes fixed on the dazzle of freedom beyond the doors.

'Joe, this is a surprise!' Professor Hau'ofa called out as he descended the stairs. His voice was genial as usual. He looked the middle-aged academic: the small black-framed spectacles softened his powerful build, his tailored sulu and sandals were casual but respectable. Behind him was DI Navala. Horseman stopped and stared, hoping his loathing didn't show.

'You must have met Joe Horseman, Detective Inspector? I have great hopes of him in tomorrow's match!'

'Really, Professor? I'm looking forward to it. Goodbye for now.'

Professor Hau'ofa made an unhurried exit and DI Navala turned to Horseman. 'I'll see you now, Mr Horseman. Let's go up to my office.'

As they climbed the stairs, possible scenarios for Coach's visit to DI Navala battled in Horseman's head. Was Coach already under suspicion? Yet both men had seemed relaxed. Had Coach cast suspicion elsewhere, perhaps on Horseman? Did the detective have any idea that he'd just shown Seru's murderer out the door with courtesy? Horseman had no idea what was afoot.

DI Navala listened with an impassive face to Horseman's revelation of the Seru-Coach-Loa triangle. 'You see, sir, it fits with Seru's diary entry and the suicide theory. But if you now think someone murdered Seru, this situation provides a motive.'

'For whom?' DI Navala asked.

Horseman was flustered, but just able to restrain himself. 'Not for me, sir. That's a judgement for you professionals. But I had to tell you because I must prove my own innocence.'

'What do you mean?'

'Yesterday Detective Sergeant Ratini told me he suspected me of killing Seru. I have to clear my name by finding out who really murdered him. If anyone did, that is.'

'Josefa, no one has to prove their innocence. On the contrary, the police must find evidence to prove a suspect is guilty. Remember that.'

'*Io*, I remember now. "Innocent until proven guilty." But is that really true? I'm under threat, so I have to do something.'

DI Navala's face grew stern. 'As I've told you before, leave this investigation to the police. We're trained and equipped to do it. You're not saving yourself, you're putting yourself in harm's way. Murderers are dangerous.'

Horseman didn't believe him. '*Io*, sir,' he said.

There was no point asking about the progress on the pathology tests, about Coach's visit or anything else. Information was a one-way street with the police, he'd learned that much this week. He'd delivered the information he considered dynamite, but this hadn't seemed to surprise DI Navala at all. Job done. But he had learned nothing in return.

18

Bindi and Horseman shared a pot of tea at a table beside the canteen's tall sash windows and waited for Loa. The breeze brought relief from the pervasive whiff of hospital disinfectant. There were other components to the cloying smell that Horseman preferred not to analyse.

He was desperate for Bindi's forgiveness, even though she'd granted him permission to pass on Loa's secret. 'So you see, Bindi, I had no choice, not only to get myself off the hook, but for Seru as well. You know, to save his reputation and to get justice for him, too.'

Bindi reached out and covered his

clenched hands with her own. Her eyes were ineffably sad. 'I know, Joe. You're a good kid. I know you'll do what you think is right.'

'Loa deserves my honesty, but I don't know how to tell her.'

'*Our* honesty, Joe. Yours and mine too. It was me who decided to break my best friend's confidence. Here's Loa now.'

Could Loa possibly have lost weight in just the last few days? Maybe it was her long dark skirt and plain blue over-blouse. But her pale face was thinner too, her brown eyes enormous. She looked ill, yet so beautiful and innocent. And he was about to destroy any trust she had given him.

Bindi poured a third mug of tea and placed it in front of Loa, who smiled gratefully. 'Thanks, Bindi, this is just what I need. We had two hours of surgical rounds, then theatre observations that ran late, as they always do. I'm glad to sit down.'

'Good. Drink your tea while you listen to us. I'm sorry, Loa, but we've both got confessions to make.'

Bindi began her halting and brief story under Loa's fixed gaze, but when Bindi referred to Loa's arrangements with the coach, Loa lowered her eyes to her tea as a red flush rose up her neck. Horseman's stomach churned while Bindi spoke and now it was his turn.

'I decided to pass on what Bindi told me to the police because DS Ratini suspects me of murdering Seru. And I have to uncover the truth about his death because Seru deserves justice. I hated being a snitch and I realise I've probably let you in for more questions from the police. I beg your forgiveness, Loa.' He gulped his tea, noticed his hand was shaking and clattered the mug down.

Loa looked up at him, teardrops rolling down her face. 'I understand all about difficult choices, Joe. I wish you hadn't gone to the police, but of course I forgive you.'

Horseman managed his first deep breath for hours. '*Vinaka vakalevu*, Loa. I'm truly grateful.' Loa smiled slightly, inclined her head to him graciously.

'Bindi, I haven't eaten all day. Could you be a dear and get me something while I go to the Ladies?'

'Sure. What would you like?'

'Anything that looks like it hasn't been sitting around all day.'

'Okay, I'll get food for all of us. There's a queue but I'll be as quick as I can. Joe, you mind our table.'

'Right, boss,' he grinned, grabbed a *Fiji Times* left on the next table and turned to the sports pages.

He'd finished the sports news and turned to the front page when Loa returned and sat down, dumping her pandanus basket beside her chair. She looked across to the canteen counter. 'Looks like Bindi's got a trayful but she's still waiting in line at the cash register.'

Horseman folded his newspaper, glad that Loa had recovered her composure but uncomfortable to be alone with her. 'I'll go and help her.'

He bounced up, shoving his chair aside

just as Loa bent to lift her own chair away from the table. Horseman righted his toppling chair, stepping on Loa's basket as he did so. Loa sat down and grabbed at her basket but one handle was now hooked under a chair leg.

'So sorry, please get up and I'll untangle it.' Horseman bent down to free the basket but Loa did not move. Their heads collided as she tugged harder at the bag. The handle snapped off, spilling contents onto the floor. He dived to retrieve Loa's scattered things from under the table; index cards, pens, a small diary, change purse. He picked up a clear ziplock bag.

'Joe, don't touch my things—I can get them.' Loa's voice was brittle, panicky.

'Sorry, sorry. Of course.' But he already had the ziplock bag in his hand. As he handed it to her he couldn't avoid registering the tiny syringes, the white box labelled *Insulin*.

Their eyes met. He couldn't fathom their meaning. She shrugged as if resigned. 'Well, now you know!'

When Bindi returned with dalo chips, chicken soup and bread, Loa silently showed her the ziplock bag before stowing it away in her broken basket. 'Tell him, please, Bindi. I don't feel up to it. I need to eat something.'

Bindi placed a deep bowl of soup in front of her friend. 'No worries, Loa. Joe, when Professor Hau'ofa diagnosed Loa with Type-1 diabetes a year ago, he hid her condition from FSM. He looked after her and no one else but Seru and I knew.'

'But why?'

'Medicine is a gruelling course and the FSM authorities require students to be in excellent health. It's understandable. Loa would probably lose her scholarship from the Tongan government and even her enrolment in the medical degree would be at risk.'

'Not that I could pay the fees anyway. Unlike other Tongan students in Fiji, I'm not high-born. My family is quite ordinary, with no cash to spare at all. But my ambition since I was a very little girl has always been to become a doctor. I don't know why. I'm the apple of my parents' eyes. They'd be crushed if I was sent home, unable to qualify. You'll understand that, Joe.' She gave him a small smile.

'Eat up, girl. These chips are quite fresh, really,' Bindi said.

Her soup finished, Loa started on the chips.

19

Loa sat in a window seat with Horseman beside her as the FSM shuttle bus pulled out of the hospital bay, heading north to the Tamavua campus. He pondered whether he had pointed the police in quite the wrong direction just a few hours ago. What he'd told them was the truth, but not the whole truth. Warnings from everyone to steer clear of the case and let the police investigate had only been sensible, he realised now. What could he contribute—a boy fresh from an outlying island of just a few villages? Nothing but loyalty to his dead hero, and even that may have been misplaced.

He recalled Coach's surprised, even sceptical reaction, when he read the list of drugs in Dr Young's report. If he had murdered Seru with insulin, maybe in combination with other drugs, surely he wouldn't have reacted like that. Of course he could easily get insulin; he'd obtained it for Loa, possibly by a normal prescription, possibly by more secret means. But the bombshell that Loa herself was insulin-dependent changed everything.

She was tired, he could see that. She gazed out the window but he didn't think she was taking in the glorious purple and orange swirls of the sunset sky. Usually so upright, her shoulders slumped. As she relaxed, her right arm and thigh pressed against his. Awkward, he edged his right buttock off the narrow seat so that she wouldn't feel pinioned. Did she feel like she was his prisoner? He didn't want that role, but didn't know what he did want.

Loa had insulin, and access to Seru's prescribed drugs. She was in an impossible situation, which he still believed was not of

her own making, but which must have
generated unendurable conflict with Seru.
Horseman didn't have a clue how Seru had
responded, but he knew he couldn't rule
out violence. The more he thought, the
more he was overwhelmed by sorrow and a
sense of futility. His eyes brimmed and he
rubbed his sleeve over his face.

He was sitting on a bus beside a
murderer and he needed to ask her one
question: why?

20

Horseman caught her just in time as she stumbled down the bus steps. 'I'm quite alright, Joe. Parasthesia, you know—my foot went to sleep on the trip, wedged against the wheel well.'

But just a few metres on she tripped on the path so Horseman offered an arm to support her. She took it but her steps were unsteady so he wrapped his arm around her waist while they made their way towards Professor Hau'ofa's house.

'Loa, I wanted to see you safely home, but you're not well, you seem exhausted. I'll come in and stay with you until you're feeling better.' She made no protest, allowing herself to be led to the sofa. Horseman strode the few steps to the kitchen bench, lit the gas ring and put the kettle on, plucked a banana from her fruit bowl and brought it to her.

'My mother's a district nurse. She told me what to do when someone with diabetes feels faint. A banana and a cup of sweet tea is her prescription. Do you agree?'

'Yes, your mother's right. *Vinaka*, Joe.' She took the banana, swung her legs up onto the sofa and stuffed a cushion behind her head.

'I don't understand. Bindi made sure you had soup and dalo chips less than an hour ago. Why are you still sick now? Shouldn't you have recovered?'

'Don't worry, Joe. I've got a headache that's made me wobbly—it's nothing. I injected insulin in the canteen toilet, but I probably needed it hours earlier. My timetable today was back-to-back, so I didn't get a break when I could test my blood sugar. I'll come good—just taking longer this time.'

Horseman made the tea and brought it over to her. Now he had the chance to ask her for an explanation, he couldn't bring himself to do so. He knew she'd killed Seru, but wanted to avoid hearing her admit it. He must stop this dithering and act.

They sipped their tea in silence for a few minutes. Eventually he blurted out the question. 'Why did you do it, Loa?'

She looked at him, then lowered her eyes in that demure way she had. 'Do what?'

'You know what I'm asking. Why did you kill Seru?' There, he'd said it, but he didn't feel any better.

She looked shocked, but then her voice rose in anger and she looked up at him, her eyes wide and blazing with hate.

'It's all your precious coach's fault. He's to blame for everything. Professor Hau'ofa killed Seru.'

Horseman was shocked. He couldn't have jumped to the wrong conclusion yet again, could he?

'From the beginning, please Loa. Tell

me what happened from the beginning.'

She seemed to exhale her outrage in a sigh and rested her head on the cushion again. She gazed at the ceiling and began.

'Well, what Bindi told you is true. I always wanted Seru, ever since I met him when I was a brand new uni student like you, Joe. Seru was a year ahead, so confident and sophisticated. He was wonderful. It took him a year to ask me on a date but not much later we were living in each other's pockets. Seru and Professor Hau'ofa were always close too. As you know, the professor loves mentoring the promising rugby players—it makes him feel he's such a good guy. When I began to feel ill last year, I had no energy at all and fell behind in my study. That was a strain on Seru. He couldn't understand the change in me. I went to the Prof—as a Med. student and a fellow Tongan, I knew he would help me.' Loa trailed off.

'Did he help you?' Horseman asked.

She leaned forward and looked him in the eyes. 'Yes, he was terrific, so clever and thoughtful. He diagnosed me correctly, explained why we should keep my condition secret from FSM and how we should do that by my moving from the dorm into his maid's flat. He trained me to manage my diabetes well and I became healthier and my marks picked up.'

Horseman let his disapproval show. 'You were ill, and he made you do his housework for him! I don't call that thoughtful!'

Loa smiled. 'Oh but it was! He said neighbours would be suspicious if a tenant student wasn't seen to be doing a job for her landlord. I've never done much housework. I hang the washing out and take it in so neighbours will notice me doing that. I mop the floors, sweep the concrete underneath the house with a coconut broom once a week and that's about it. Really, it wouldn't even be ten hours a week, probably five or six.'

'Oh well, that's all right then.'

Loa ignored the sarcasm. 'Yes, it was. Until things changed.'

Horseman steeled himself for what was to come.

'We became close, with all these secrets. But then, he fell in love with me and when his wife decided to stay in Tonga this year, he couldn't restrain himself any longer.'

'Couldn't?'

'No. I had no interest in him, he's old enough to be my father and he's running to fat!' She shuddered. 'But I liked him and was so grateful to him, how could I refuse?'

'Loa, Professor Hau'ofa broke every rule in the book! He criminally exploited you as both a patient and a student!'

Loa shook her head, smiling. 'That's all very well in theory, Joe. Real life isn't like that. Especially here in the Pacific islands. Seru soon found out and was deeply hurt. I begged him to help me end it with Prof. Stand up to him somehow. I suggested he threaten to resign from the team, or report Prof to FSM. Seru refused, actually refused! He claimed that the threats were meaningless, as he could only be on the team until his final exams in a few months anyway. Unless he failed, but Seru never fails.' Bitterness edged into her voice.

'As for reporting him to FSM for sexual harassment, Seru reckoned that was an empty threat too, because Prof had risked a lot to protect me and my scholarship. He could simply do what he should have done in the first place; refer me for treatment to the specialist clinic.'

Horseman agreed with Seru's argument, while understanding that Loa felt betrayed.

'How could he choose the Prof over me? After we'd loved each other for years? How could he make love to me, knowing that old man was doing the same? Well, I guess he couldn't, because since then he lost his passion. He excused himself with pressures of study, the team, sore joints – anything! But I think it was some kind of twisted respect for his beloved coach. Like I said, Prof is completely responsible for what happened.'

She had worked herself up to a temper now. Is this what love entailed? Horseman hoped not. Now he was starting to understand *why*, he needed to know *how*.

'Loa, how did you manage it with Seru?'

'I never stooped to stealing drugs or deceiving a doctor or pharmacist. I would quite rightly be expelled for such unethical actions. I simply consistently took less insulin than I should have and saved it up. That's another reason I haven't been so well the last few months. I was so upset last Sunday night when Seru told me again he couldn't pressure the Prof to give me up— what he meant was that he wouldn't! He spent the night here. I couldn't sleep, I couldn't take it any more, so I injected the insulin into his buttock as he slept.'

'Didn't he wake up?'

'No, he stirred then settled again. The needles are very fine, you hardly feel them. Seru's a heavy sleeper and he was in awful pain from a shoulder injury so he took codeine as well as ibuprofen…'

'I did some reading last night—it seems many adults survive an overdose of insulin. The effect on an individual is quite unpredictable. Why did you choose insulin anyway?'

Loa frowned. 'Why were you reading up on insulin, Joe?'

Damn, he shouldn't be giving her information, but he couldn't come up with any other explanation than the truth. 'Oh, Dr Young's latest results show insulin in Seru's samples.'

'Really? My textbook claims that insulin is undetectable in blood after quite a short time.'

'Maybe it wasn't blood. I don't know any more about it Loa.'

'Joe, I never meant for Seru to die! How could you think that? I was so hurt that I just wanted him to suffer—maybe miss a game. I see now I was being spiteful, wanting to punish him for not loving me enough. I must have been mad.'

Horseman's heart raced as he stared at her, horrified. Some colour had revitalised her lovely face. She sat erect, reached up and pulled off the hair clasp, letting the black waves cascade down her back and over her breasts.

He was dead scared of gaining further

insights into Loa's actions. An inner voice urged him to call the police, but in the end, he ignored it. What evidence was there? She could easily deny what she'd just told him. However, he needed to decide what to do if evidence did come his way. His indecision disturbed him.

21

'You're a good person, Joe. I trust you and I know you'd never betray my trust. And there's not a scrap of evidence that what I told you is true. Is there?'

'Are you starting to feel better? I'll pour you another cup of tea.' Loa's smile was weak but she nodded.

She was stretched out on the sofa once more, her head resting on the cushion when he returned from the kitchen. Her eyes were shut. Alarmed, he dropped the cup. Thank God, Loa was clear of the scalding liquid that poured down his cargo pants and the dozens of ceramic shards that bounced off the tiled floor. She sat up, her eyes wide open. 'What happened?'

'Don't worry, Loa, it's just a broken cup and spilt tea. My fault, I'm sorry. You stay where you are. Where can I find a mop or floorcloth?'

'Oh, there's a broom cupboard in the bathroom. Thank you, Joe.' Her sleepy voice trailed off as she leaned back on her cushion again.

He rushed to the bathroom, grabbed a wash cloth from a hook beside the sink, sponged the tea from his clothes and leg with cold water. He'd have some blisters but he'd survive. As he glanced in the mirror, he noticed a bright yellow box on the shelf with the familiar adhesive sticker: *Sharps*. His mother issued a box just like this to every insulin-dependent diabetic patient. He lifted it and jiggled it. It was pretty full. The syringe that injected Seru with insulin four days ago could well be inside. If it was, maybe it would be possible for Dr Young to identify it. That would be evidence, wouldn't it?

He got a bucket, mop, dustpan and

handbrush from the neat broom cupboard and returned to the mess by the sofa. While Loa seemed to doze, he cleaned it all up and dumped everything on the front verandah. He'd rinse and wring the mop out later.

Horseman sat in the chair opposite Loa. How could he hand this beautiful killer to the police? And why did he think of her as a killer anyway? After all, he was no expert; he didn't really know what happened. He didn't know whether the insulin had killed Seru, or was only partly responsible as one of several drugs in his system. Perhaps the insulin had nothing to do with Seru's death. He had no responsibility to the police, who'd constantly told him to mind his own business and leave the investigation to them. Well, he should follow their advice.

But another argument was nagging him. The only reason he was here now was because he'd vowed to clear Seru's name, and later his own, by finding out the truth about how Seru died. Now he'd found the truth, or at least a key to it, neither he nor Seru would be exonerated unless the police knew about it too. Justice could prevail only if it was blind.

He noticed Loa's face had paled even more, and bluish smudges darkened the delicate skin around her eyes. Maybe she wasn't asleep, maybe she was unconscious. Panicking, he jumped up and shook her shoulder. She opened her exhausted eyes. 'What, why are you here?' She looked around as if confused by her surroundings. Suddenly he understood.

'Loa, why are you still not taking enough insulin? I've been with you for a couple of hours; you've had food, drink and a rest, but you haven't recovered. You must still be going short on insulin.'

'What? Are you a doctor now?'

'Loa, you know far more than I do. But I do know a bit because my grandfather had diabetes, my mother's a district nurse and she taught me how to look after him.'

She smiled and sank back on the cushion.

'Tell me Loa, why aren't you taking your insulin?'

He could see her struggling to concentrate. 'What? Oh, I see. I'm saving it up, I told you.'

'What for, Loa?'

'For Seru's killer. It won't be a problem. He's a very heavy sleeper.'

She laid her head down again. The next moment they heard pounding on the door, and Professor Hau'ofa burst in, looking round wildly.

'Joe, Joe, what are you doing here? I told you to butt out and I meant it! Get out at once! You have no place here! You are not wanted!' He flung out his arm, pointing at the open door and the darkness beyond.

Coach's fury evaporated as his gaze embraced Loa. The sight of her smoothed his features and relaxed his tense body. He went to her, supported her head with one huge hand, taking her pulse with the other, speaking to her all the while in Tongan. Although Horseman didn't know Tongan at all, he could understand what Coach's words expressed. They were gentle yet passionate, comforting yet anxious. Loa was right: Coach was in love with her.

While Coach continued to implore Loa, Horseman retreated to the kitchen bench and the telephone. No, he couldn't call the police, not yet. Then it came to him—Dr Young! He would know what to do. If the doctor chose to call for the police, so be it. He lifted the handset and dialled the number as quietly as he could. Damn! A recorded message at the lab gave an emergency number.

'Dr Matthew Young.' Thank goodness.

'Doctor, it's Joe Horseman. Loa injected Seru with insulin. She's here, in her flat at Professor Hau'ofa's house at FSM. She's ill, Professor Hau'ofa has just arrived. Please come now!'

'Right, mate. You stay safe, I'm calling the police, then I'll be with you.'

He didn't need to put the phone down quietly. Loa raised her voice, shouting in rapid Tongan, ignoring the coach's soothing entreaties. Horseman took a few steps towards the sofa, unsure whether to intervene. He couldn't understand what they were saying, so how could he help? Loa had revived, at least for now. She struggled against Coach's firm grip on her arms. He was calm, using just enough force to restrain her, but no more. That's how it looked to Horseman. He couldn't do Loa any good by tackling the coach and he could easily inflame the conflict.

Thank goodness, Loa soon calmed down and Coach released her. She eased her legs off the sofa and the older man sat beside her stroking her shoulder, still speaking softly. They ignored Horseman, or were oblivious to him. He prayed that Dr Young would get here soon—this situation was way out of his league and much too much responsibility. Bindi called him *kid* affectionately, but that's all he was.

Loa reached for her pandanus basket which Horseman had dumped beside the sofa when he'd helped her into the flat. She dragged it in front of her and fumbled inside with both hands, feeling for something.

The ziplock insulin injecting pack? Why

hadn't he twigged when Loa said she was saving insulin for Seru's killer? Horseman edged forward to the back of the sofa in time to glimpse the syringe protruding from her curled hand as she withdrew it slowly from the bag. He reached over to grip her wrist. Too late, her hand darted behind her back. Professor Hau'ofa sprang up and shouted one word—'Loa'. He tried to wrestle the syringe from her hand but Loa was lightning quick. She passed the syringe to her left hand and lunged at the professor, who dodged her weapon. She screamed with rage. As Horseman seized her arms from behind, she twisted her body and jabbed back. She stabbed the syringe through Horseman's tee-shirt into his abdomen and drove in the plunger. He felt the drug forcing its way into his flesh. He wondered what it would do to him. It was his own fault—he could easily have restrained her but he couldn't bring himself to hurt her; she who was so ill.

Her violent fit spent, Loa held her head in her hands then slid to the floor. Coach pulled the syringe from Horseman's belly. 'Don't worry, Joe, you'll be okay. I'll just settle Loa first. Bring some water.' He half-lifted her onto the sofa again, coaxing her to sip the water Horseman brought. He lifted her legs up and lay her head on the cushion. She closed her eyes.

'I'll test her blood sugar now.' He plucked a device from her ziplock bag and pricked a finger. He frowned at the gauge, cracked open an insulin dose and injected it into her abdomen. 'There, she'll be okay in a while. Best to let her rest and revive naturally. Her system didn't take the strain of the last few days well, I'm afraid.'

Horseman wondered what was happening to his own system. Was it the insulin making his head swim or was he imagining it?

'Sit yourself down, Joe. I'll get you something to eat and you'll be right as rain.' Horseman wasn't sure he should trust Coach but he was so used to obeying him he flopped into the armchair. Coach rifled through the kitchen cupboards and returned with a packet of coconut biscuits. He ripped it open and placed it in Horseman's lap. 'Get as many of these into you as you can. I need you for the game tomorrow.'

Dr Young appeared in the doorway, scanning the scene. 'Everything under control here now? Professor, can I help? I've brought my bag of tricks.' He turned to show them a bulging backpack but didn't take it off.

'Police! Nobody move, nobody move! Stay where you are, stay where you are!' All four of them froze at DS Ratini's angry shouts. Four officers appeared, truncheons drawn, then the detective, his pistol pointing at the ceiling.

Professor Hau'ofa spoke first. 'Detective Sergeant, Dr Young and I are treating two medical emergencies here. The situation is calm, so please let us continue.'

A constable shut the door on a couple of neighbours who had rushed up to see what was going on. Ratini lowered his pistol and glowered at Dr Young. 'Doctor, you alerted us to a violent situation here.'

'I arrived just a minute ago, Detective Sergeant, at the urgent request of young Joe Horseman here, as you know. The situation is now under control. When Joe's fit, he's the best person to relate this evening's events.'

SATURDAY

22

Two uniformed constables drove Professor Hau'ofa to Albert Park, precisely an hour before the game was due to kick off. The waiting USP players were surprised but none of them thought too much about it and Horseman wasn't going to fill anyone in. They'd play better if they knew nothing about what had happened last night up at Tamavua. He had to hand it to Coach, who behaved just as he always did—reviewing overall strategy and tactics, reminding them of Police players' weaknesses, psyching them all up, as if nothing had changed. Then, just before they ran on to the field, he declared, 'This game is for Seru, the greatest USP captain ever. Make him proud, boys! Show him what you can do! Win!'

USP lost, as everyone expected. The absence of the USP captain and star player meant that the tougher and more experienced Police team won by a punishing margin. Afterwards, Coach had astonished the team by praising their tenacity. 'Next time you play Police, you'll score better and I know you'll end up beating them. I want to thank you, team, for all you've given me. I'm sorry to tell you I may not see you for some time. I have to go to Tonga on a family matter. Until I return, my colleague Sitiveni Vula will keep you up to the mark and beyond. Your next training session will be on Monday afternoon as usual.'

The hovering uniforms nodded. Professor Hau'ofa strolled with them to the waiting police car.

When Horseman emerged from the changing rooms under the stand, the kit bags hanging from his shoulders, a tall figure waited beyond the clusters of bewildered students. Horseman called farewells to his team mates and approached Detective Inspector Navala.

'*Bula*, Josefa. You played well. I see you could present a threat to Police in future.'

'*Vinaka*, sir. Police deserve their reputation as the toughest team.' He paused, awkward. 'Do you want to interview me again, sir?'

'*Io*, but not now. The statement you made this morning has been typed up and ready for you to check and sign. But you'll be tired. If you drop in to the station on Monday morning, that will be fine.'

'I know it's not my business, but how is Loa?'

'She's recovering in the specialist diabetes unit at the hospital. The Tongan High Commissioner has notified me that when she's stabilised, she'll be moving in with his family for a while. He must know Fiji has an extradition treaty with Tonga, so she won't be immune from prosecution under his roof. He's probably just trying to look after her.'

'Have you charged her, sir?'

'Not yet, no. Do you think she should be charged?'

'I don't know. What does Dr Young have to say?'

'Aha, you've zeroed in on the key question, Josefa. Well done. You deserve to know that Dr Young finalised his post mortem report this afternoon. He concludes that Seru died from a combination of toxins in his system. So, while insulin contributed to Seru's death, it's impossible to allocate proportional responsibility to the different toxins.'

Horseman persisted. He had to know. 'But would Seru have died if she hadn't given him insulin?'

'No, he wouldn't. Dr Young was clear about that in his report.'

'Loa told me insulin couldn't be detected in blood. Was she wrong?'

'No, she was right there. No trace remains after quite a short time. Dr Young found an injection site and tested the tissue around it. That's the current technique, he told me. It took a few days, but he found a high concentration of insulin. However, as Loa denies any intention to kill Seru, it's unlikely that a murder or even a manslaughter charge could be sustained. It might come down to assault and grievous bodily harm. However, she did quite deliberately save up insulin over a period of months by underdosing herself. I imagine the prosecutor would give that fact a great deal of weight.' DI Navala looked thoughtful.

'Will she be able to continue her studies, sir? She wants to be a doctor more than anything. She just made one mistake.'

'It was a big one, though, wasn't it? A big one indeed. It's not for me to decide about continuing her studies, Josefa. It's early days, early days in the criminal legal process. Strange things can happen there. But ask yourself, would you trust a doctor who did what she's done?'

Horseman looked down, feeling helpless. DI Navala had made a fair point, but he was haunted by Loa's face as she entreated him to understand. Then a laughing Seru invaded his mind. Super-talented Seru, headed for success, whose life was snatched away. He'd been Horseman's idol, but the last few days had uncovered his feet of clay.

'Get in touch with me if you have any more questions or thoughts. You've played an important part in this case and I know you'll want to follow it through.'

'*Vinaka*, sir.'

'I mean it. You asked good questions and kept asking. You showed persistence. You never let go of the ball. By the way, how keen are you on your Business course?'

Horseman shifted his feet. This was something he'd been wondering about recently. How had DI Navala known? 'Hard to say, sir. I'm only in my first year. My father's an accounts clerk—he thinks the degree will provide me with plenty of work choices. But I really don't know what I want to do after I graduate.'

'Hmm. You strike me as a young man who's more interested in justice than making money. Keep in mind that it's much easier to investigate a crime from inside the police force, with the right training and resources.'

'I hadn't thought about it like that, sir.'

'Think about it, Josefa. Think about it. Give me a call after you graduate, or before, if you decide Business Studies is not for you. *Moce.*'

'*Vinaka*, sir. I'll think about it. *Moce.*' He set off for the bus stop but had only gone a few metres when DI Navala called his name. Horseman turned.

'Another fact to bear in mind, Josefa. Police will always field a stronger rugby team than USP. Always!'

EXCLUSIVE GIFT FOR
MY READERS

I trust you enjoyed finding out how young Joe Horseman turned to a life of crime. Like readers of my full-length novels in the **Fiji Islands Mysteries** series, you may have equally enjoyed discovering Fiji. I was privileged to live and work in these fascinating islands in the first decade of this century. Indeed, my motivation to embark on my **Fiji Islands Mysteries** was to share my love for these beautiful islands and their inhabitants.

When I published **Death on Paradise Island**, I began a blog which has evolved to include Fijian food, customs, history, sport…whatever occurs to me. I've been so delighted with the responses to my posts, I have now compiled the best into a slim illustrated volume. *Finding Fiji* is a short, selective, subjective collection of snippets that is far from comprehensive. However, I believe readers may gain fresh insights into the island nation from this little book.

Finding Fiji is not available from retailers. but is exclusive to members of B.M. Allsopp's Readers. So I invite you to join us today. Each month, I'll write to you with a snippet about Fiji and the latest freebies in crime fiction. You'll always be the first to know about my new releases too.

As a welcome gift, I'll present you with *Finding Fiji!*

Get your free copy at www.bmallsopp.com

ENJOY THIS BOOK? YOU CAN MAKE A BIG DIFFERENCE.

As an indie author, I don't have the financial muscle of a major world publisher behind me. What I do have is loyal readers who loved my first books and took the trouble to post reviews online. These reviews brought my book to the attention of other readers.

I would be most grateful if you could spend just five minutes posting a short review on Amazon, Goodreads or your favourite book review site.

ACKNOWLEDGEMENTS

I am grateful to many people who helped me with this book. First I owe thanks to Mr Waisea Vakamocea, retired senior officer of the Fiji Police Force, who patiently answered my questions. Responsibility for errors relating to police procedure in this book is all mine.

Second, I am most grateful to the expert professionals who transformed my manuscript into a real book. Editor Irina Dunn gave me perceptive advice. Polgarus Studios designed and formatted the text with flair and Maryna Zhukova of MaryDes once more created the cover of my dreams.

I am indebted to the volunteer advance readers of Horseman's Cavalry who eliminated many errors and reassured me that they enjoyed the story.

Finally, I thank Peter Williamson for his eagle eye through several rounds of proof reading, his enthusiasm for my writing and constant support.

ABOUT THE AUTHOR

B.M. Allsopp is the author of the *Fiji Islands Mysteries* series. She lived in the South Pacific islands for fourteen years, including four in Fiji, where she taught at the University of the South Pacific in Suva. She now lives in Sydney with her husband and tabby cat. You're always welcome at her online home: www.bmallsopp.com.

ALSO BY B.M. ALLSOPP

Death on Paradise Island: Fiji Islands Mysteries 1

An island paradise. A grisly murder. Can a detective put his rugby days behind him to tackle a killer case?

Josefa "Joe" Horseman holds out hope for a comeback. But after riding high in top class rugby, returning to the Fiji detective force with a bum knee and a promotion-hungry new partner wasn't what he had in mind. So he knows he'll have to up his game when guests at an island resort discover a young maid's corpse snagged on the reef.

Sorting through the victim's list of jealous admirers, Horseman's under pressure to solve the case before the high-end vacation spot takes a major hit to its reputation… and its bottom line. But just as he uncovers a lead on a sabotage suspect, another body rises to the surface.

Can Horseman bring down the killer before the waters run red with more blood?

Reader reviews for Death on Paradise Island

'I'm pretty sure I'll never get to the Fiji islands, so thanks for bringing them to me.' - *Amazon*

'Please get writing the next installment! I look forward to hearing more about Joe, his deputies, the street boys, the food and the beautiful islands so far away from Connecticut!' - *Amazon*

'It was perfect entertainment!' - *Amazon*

To buy, go to www.bmallsopp.com/books

Death by Tradition: Fiji Islands Mysteries 2

Must DI Joe Horseman sacrifice his chance at love to catch a killer?

Only 5 more days… Horseman can't wait for Melissa, his American girlfriend, to join him in Fiji. This time, he wants love to last.

So, when a young activist is murdered at Tanoa in the remote highlands, Horseman sets a deadline to crack the case. Too close a deadline, for Tanoa is beyond radio reach. What's more, the villagers are steeped in the old ways and cannot be hurried, so Horseman and Sergeant Susie Singh must navigate both the back roads and the minefield of Fijian custom with care. As Horseman counts the hours to Melissa's touch down, he has no idea of the dangers looming through the mountain mist.

Death by Tradition is the second release in the *Fiji Islands Mysteries series*. Crime fans who hanker after exotic settings will love

B.M. Allsopp's disturbing whodunit.

Reader reviews for Death by Tradition
'Second book in this series and I enjoyed it as much if not more than the first. I absolutely loved the Fijian setting. I think Fiji just moved up a couple notches on my "Must do" list.' – *Goodreads*

'Above all, this is an exciting, enjoyable, well-written murder mystery.' - *Amazon*

To buy, go to www.bmallsopp.com/books

Death Beyond the Limit: Fiji Islands Mysteries 3

Can a landlubber detective combat evil on the high seas?

Inspector Joe Horseman stares into the eyes of a severed head. Fished out of a shark's gut, the unknown victim is soon dubbed *Jona* by the media. Did the tiger shark kill Jona or was he already dead when it clamped its teeth around his neck? Horseman must battle ruthless criminals, bureaucracy and even the law itself to dredge up the answers.

But cracking the case may not be enough. Can Horseman stop this crime sinking without trace in the lawless ocean?

Death Beyond the Limit is the third novel in the exotic **Fiji Islands Mysteries** series. Mystery lovers who like diving deep into turbulent waters will love B.M. Allsopp's gut-wrenching investigation.

Advance readers' praise for Death Beyond the Limit
'A genuinely great read!'
'The relentless pursuit kept me captivated.'
'So many twists and turns that I did not see coming.'

To buy, go to www.bmallsopp.com/books